BIG DEAL

Also in this series

STRIKERS

BIG DEAL

DAVID ROSS AND BOB CATTELL

MADCAP

First published in Great Britain in 1999
by Madcap Books,
André Deutsch Ltd,
76 Dean St,
London, W1V 5HA
www.vci.co.uk

André Deutsch is a subsidiary of VCI plc

A catalogue record for this title is available from the
British Library

ISBN 0 233 99509 9

Printed by Mackays of Chatham plc

3 5 7 9 10 8 6 4 2

Bob Cattell was born in East Anglia in 1948 and now
lives in North London. He combines his job as an
advertising copywriter with writing children's books
about sport. He is a lifelong Aston Villa supporter.

David Ross was somehow always the reserve in his
school football team, which gave him lots of time to
observe the game. He loves to hate supporting Heart
of Midlothian and has written numerous other books
for children.

CHAPTER ONE

TEAM TALK

'It's too much! I can't take it.'

Thomas Headley pressed his hands against his ears. His mobile phone was ringing. His mother was holding up the office phone to him. He couldn't hear what she was saying because the front-door bell was chiming and a CD player was throbbing away in the next room. His little brother, Richie, was pulling at his elbow. Thomas yanked himself away and went to the window. From the other side of the garden hedge, a figure popped up, pointing a lightweight TV camera at him. With a furious tug he snapped the curtains shut. The room was plunged into darkness.

'Hey!'

'Put the light on!'

'Thomas, it's Joss. You must speak to him.' It was his mother's voice, piercing through Richie's indignant shouts.

'You speak to him, Elaine.'

'Come on, Thomas, you can't hide from it forever,' said Elaine, who was Thomas's business manager as well as being his mother.

He reached over with a sigh and took the phone. 'Yeah?'

'Thomas?' The deep, familiar tones of Sherwood Strikers' manager sounded in his ear. 'Listen, son. You and I need to talk. Not at the Club. Not at your house. We'll have a car at your door in twenty minutes. Just get in it, if you know what's good for you. What's the time now? Be ready by eleven. See you then.'

'Yeah, but . . .'

The phone went dead. Joss Morecombe had rung off. Thomas retreated to his bedroom, an airy, comfortable upstairs room with its own big-screen TV and computer system. He slumped into a large, shiny red armchair.

'I've had enough,' he said aloud to himself. In his hand he still held a copy of the new, three-year contract with Sherwood Strikers that Elaine wanted him to sign. He screwed it up in a tight little ball and threw it across the room. Then he sat waiting for eleven o'clock.

The getaway was beautifully directed. The car that came to fetch him was a stretched, dark-windowed Daimler limo. Two burly men cleared a path past the crowd of journalists and cameras.

'Thomas, what are your plans?' shouted someone. 'Are you leaving Sherwood? Where are you going?'

'Give us a statement, Thomas!' shouted another.

Cameras flashed. Thomas slid into the back

seat of the Daimler and the door clicked shut. He found himself next to Joss Morecombe. Joss was wearing a heavy black overcoat and his broad-rimmed Italian hat was pressed down on his mane of long white hair. He nodded at Thomas. The limo eased away and, as it cleared the end of the exclusive tree-bordered street, a plain green mini-cab drove out and blocked the way. The two burly men climbed into it. The pressmen who had leapt for their cars were blocked off by the grinning cab driver, and could only watch the tail of the Daimler swinging away into the distance.

'Lucky, that cab,' said Thomas, looking back.

'Lucky my armpit,' said Joss Morecombe. 'D'you think I've never had to do this before? That mini-cab driver is my old pal Mossy Stones. We were at primary school together. He's practically on the Strikers' payroll.'

Thomas opened his mouth to speak, but the big man made a commanding gesture. 'Keep it for now. Enjoy the ride. We're not going far.'

The Shoemaker's Arms at Maxted – once a village pub, now a luxury country inn – was the destination. Joss was expected. They entered by a side door and were directed to a sitting room in a private suite. A huge pot of tea and a pile of Joss's trademark ham-and-mustard-and-cress sandwiches arrived almost immediately. At last Joss spoke. 'So tell me. What's up, lad?'

'Well, I'm not sure. It's this new contract. I'm not really . . .'

Joss listened in silence and Thomas struggled

on. 'I mean . . . three years is a long time and the thing is . . . I think I want a transfer.'

'And I want to hop to Southampton on a pogo-stick,' Joss replied smiling. 'Tell me what's really up, Thomas. No hurry. I've got all day.'

'It's everything about this place,' said Thomas. 'I can't walk down the street any more. Everyone's after me. Girls scream at me. People push me around in pubs. I get no peace at home. The phone never stops ringing. There's always someone after me to do things. Sign footballs for raffles. Open their stupid pizza restaurant for free. Play a charity golf day. Abseil down the StaWest's head office. Invest my money for me. Interview me. It never stops.'

'I thought your mum . . . er . . . Elaine looked after all that.'

'She does. But I'm the one who has to go out and be photographed and pushed around by so-called fans. I want to play football. And I don't like being got at all the time.'

'Who's getting at you?'

Thomas was silent.

'Could it be our sharp-tongued little friend, Drew Stilton?'

Still no answer.

'Would it surprise you to know that he's complained to me about you?'

'WHAT?'

Joss smiled again and offered Thomas another sandwich. 'Go on, take two. They're good.' Thomas wasn't hungry but he reached out to the plate Joss was holding. 'Drew says you freeze him out on the field. He's the last person you'll pass the ball to. A bit of truth in that, isn't there?'

Thomas felt himself growing hot. 'Yeah, well. He never stops trying to wind me up, all the time . . . like when he hid my new Nike boots when I had that photo-call with them. Or when he . . .' Thomas's voice slowed down and then stopped altogether. All of a sudden Drew Stilton's endless mockery which had been making his life a misery seemed small and petty.

Joss held up his hands. 'Okay, I know you boys are never going to be best mates. But listen, Thomas, you needn't let Drew get to you. He's not much more than a clever pair of feet and – between you and me – a peanut-sized brain. You've got a head on your shoulders, son. It's with players like you that we're building the club's future. You're what I would call a real foot-baller.'

Thomas knew he had just been paid the great-est compliment of his life, but he still felt confused and angry.

'I blame myself for this,' said Joss. 'I took my eye off the ball and didn't see the pressure you were under. Some lads hit the bottle – you just bottle it up. But don't worry, I've dealt with it before. First, no more interviews, no more chasing you for quotes. I'll pass the word around. Any journalist who wants to see the inside of the Strikers' hospitality suite again isn't going to ignore that. The club will give you full protection until you're ready to handle the publicity wingdings again. And, don't forget, you've got good mates in the club, haven't you? Jason? Rory? There's always safety in numbers, when you go out for a bit of relaxation. As for Master Drew Stilton – I'm afraid you've got to handle him yourself. If I tell him to lay off, it'll only sharpen his needle.'

Thomas nodded.

'You see, son, I want to keep you,' continued Joss. 'But I need Drew too. You've heard it from me before. It can take a funny mix of people to make a team that works on the field. That boy's got skill. Maybe he can't make and create quite like you but he sure as hell can put the goals away . . . if he gets enough of the action, that is.'

Joss bit deeply into a sandwich. 'Now listen,' he said through a mouthful of white bread and ham. 'I'm gonna try something different with you. I'm putting you into the back four on Saturday.'

Thomas's eyes opened wide and he was on the point of jumping up in protest when Joss spoke again.

'Wait, hear me out. What's your weight now?'

'82 kilos.'

'Height?'

'Six foot. But, Boss – I don't want to play at the back. Defence isn't my thing. I love it on the wing, or in midfield – in fact, what I really want . . .'

'I know. I know. But trust me. I do have some experience of what I'm talking about. You've grown up a lot since we bought you. You're a better footballer. But you've also grown in height, thickened out. You're not quite as fast as you were – but you're a lot stronger – you can tackle hard and you're a fine passer of the ball. A spell at the back could be just right for you.'

'I'm as fast as Jason or Big Mac,' protested Thomas.

'Maybe,' said Joss. 'But remember I've seen kids as good as you come and go – burned out on ambition or high living or both. I want you to survive and reach the very top, Thomas.'

He stared hard into into Thomas's eyes. 'All right, I'll level with you. We've got problems at the back which the top teams can exploit. Dave Franchi and Ben El Harra are a touch injury-prone. Oldie's a menace because he keeps getting suspended and, of the subs and reserves, only Tarquin Kelly has really made the step up. We need to strengthen the squad with a couple of quality defenders. I've got the money to buy them, but it takes more than money to make a football team; you need the right people. You're the obvious choice as a stop-gap. But I think it will be good for your football too. What do you say, Thomas. Is it a deal?'

The reply came almost as a sigh. 'Okay.'

'As for that new contract, Thomas, you can tear it up. You trust us, we'll trust you. And maybe at the end of the season, we'll make you an even better offer.'

'Okay.'

'And no more phone calls to to the hacks telling

them you're unhappy at Strikers and want a transfer, right? No wonder they're persecuting you. You cost me over three million quid, Thomas. And just being signed by Strikers has made you worth maybe double that. You might say you owe something to the club – a little bit of loyalty.'

On the way back in the big limo with Joss, Thomas felt strangely relieved of a burden. The talk with Joss had changed his feelings about the club and he was a bit ashamed that he'd put it about that he wasn't happy there any more. But there were still a lot of things to sort out. That smart-arse Drew for a start. And then there was the business about being played at the back. He wasn't a clogging defender. Still, it was true enough that he was slower than a year ago. He'd put on some weight and that little creep-face Drew could now beat him over fifty metres. Thomas sighed.

The limo swished along smoothly. As they turned in among the big houses of Nutberry Gardens, he saw that the little crowd of journalists and hangers-on had disappeared from his front gate. A policeman was standing casually by the corner of the road. Thomas looked at Joss and the big man shrugged his shoulders. 'Strikers is the biggest thing this city has got,' he said. 'Don't let anyone tell you I can't get results when I put my mind to it.'

CHAPTER TWO

AT THE BACK

There was nowhere to beat the atmosphere at Trent Park at three o'clock on a Saturday afternoon. Some said that the re-designed, all-seater stadium wasn't like the noisy old days of the Mound at the Park end, where all the regulars congregated and you stood up squeezed together like sardines. The Trent Park roar from the Mound of old was famous throughout the land. The ground held 85,000 then but now the capacity was well under 60,000.

But the skipper, Jamie 'Big Mac' MacLachlan didn't have much time for nostalgia. He'd seen Strikers play as a lad. 'Ach, mon, it's better the noo,' he said to Thomas. 'Yon old stadium was jist a shoogly auld tin shed. Concrete hauds in the noise, ye can really feel them cheerin ye oan.'

'Oh ah,' said Thomas, never quite sure if he understood Mac's broad Scots accent. He liked the Strikers' stadium. It wrapped round you and you felt almost snug, standing there on the turf with the massive tiers of seating rising up all round in a great oval. But today Thomas was feeling anything but snug – finding himself positioned on the left of the back four. In front of him, also out on the left today, was Drew Stilton. Curtis Cropper had the lone striker role in the absence of Ashleigh Coltrane who was out with a calf injury.

As ever, Thomas felt a tightening in his stomach as the whistle blew to start the game. The opposition, Mersey United, were level-pegging with Strikers in the Premier League, but their recent away form was poor. Nonetheless Thomas knew that the Demons – as United were known – like Sherwood, were pressing for a place in Europe, and they'd fight all the way to get there.

Thomas stretched his hamstrings – both of them had given him a bit of bother this season. He stared at his opposite number, Carl Larson, the United winger. He was the player Len Dallal, Strikers' chief coach, had told him to mark. 'He's quick but you've got to stick to him like chewing gum to a blanket, laddie,' said old Doolally. Thomas may have been a rookie defender but Len had been putting him through his paces all week. And, away from the training sessions, there had been tactics planned out on the board and endless videos of Mersey United's recent games. He'd seen quite enough of Carl Larson on the screen, but now here was the real thing.

The Striker's line-up today was to be either 4–3–3 or 4–5–1, depending on whether they were going forward or defending:

1
Sean Pincher

2   3   5   7
Dave Franchi Ben El Harra Dean Oldie Thomas Headley

8   6   4
Cosimo Lagattello Jamie MacLachlan Brad Trainor

11   20
Haile Reifer Drew Stilton

18
Curtis Cropper

The game started easily enough for Thomas. The
play was all in the United half for the first five
minutes. But then a loose cross was intercepted
and punted up-field. Big Mac rose to head it
between two United players but was pushed in
the back. The ref didn't notice the foul and the
Demons got the ball out to the wing where Larson
was lurking. He suddenly seemed to burst into
life showing amazing pace off the blocks.
Shouting across to his team-mates, he took the
ball swiftly and confidently down the right wing
with Thomas shadowing him on the inside.
Suddenly, Thomas saw a typical United build-up
plan – he'd spotted it on the videos. Their number
ten was running on for the one-two with Larson
and two other forwards were descending on the
far post for the cross. The Strikers' defence was
stretched; it was four against three. Thomas saw
Carl Larson look up and he timed his tackle
perfectly, hooking the ball out from under his feet

at the moment the pass was to be delivered. He got back to his feet and had the ball under control in one movement; then he threaded a perfect pass down the wing to Drew Stilton.

'Guid man, Tommeh,' shouted MacLachlan. 'Whit a steal! Nice one.'

Soon the game settled down to a trial of strength. There wasn't a lot of finesse about the Demons' midfield but all Strikers' early runs at goal foundered on a rock-hard defence. Thomas found himself drifting up-field a bit too often and old Doolally was constantly galloping up to the touchline to wave him back. Only once did Carl Larson get past him to the dead-ball line and then he put a poor cross into the side netting. At half time the score was 0–0 and the match had all the makings of a stalemate.

'It's gonna be a tough second half,' said Len. 'These boys play a physical game. You'll need every ounce of concentration and fitness.'

'You don't say,' murmured Curtis Cropper, who was tenderly testing a bruised calf with his finger-tips.

'I want to see the big fellas pull their weight this half,' said Len. 'Know what I mean?' His eyes flashed across to Thomas, Dean Oldie, and Dave Franchi. 'But take it easy, Deano. You know that ref and he knows you, so watch it. Keep those elbows down. No nonsense, eh?' Deano flashed his few teeth in a typical 'Psycho' grin. Psycho was just one of his many nicknames and the one which suited him best, Thomas thought –

although he was strangely fond of the mad Dean Oldie.

The buzzer went and the team got to their feet. 'You're doing good, son,' Doolally said as he tapped Thomas on the shoulder. 'But don't get caught too far up. It's okay to go on a dart up the wing once in a while but make sure you're covered. It's my guess they'll test you this half. They know Deano's a hard man and you're the new boy. I've told young Brad to back you up if you're put under pressure.'

It did not take Thomas long to realize just what Len meant. With the West End behind him echoing to the howls of the Demons' fans, suddenly it seemed that the entire United team was coming at him like a stampeding herd. United usually played in red, like Sherwood, but today they were in their away strip of light blue and dark blue stripes. And the blue tide kept coming. Larson and the number ten, Druitt, made surge after surge down the right and Thomas began to wonder which blue shirt he should mark. And when their big Finnish wing back, Turveinen, came into the picture too, he was completely thrown. Drew should have dropped back to take on the Finn but he wasn't going to help Thomas out. He was a striker, after all, not a bone-head defender.

The endless running to cut off the forward darts of the Demons down the left was taking its toll on Thomas's stamina. And when he picked up the ball and ran with it the big Finn was all too ready to dump him on the turf. After one heavy, clattering tackle he muttered something to Thomas in Finnish. It might have been 'Sorry', but it sounded more like 'Tough'. The referee looked round, too late. Thomas looked for the assistant referee's flag but he was miles away from the action.

The whistle went for a handball ten yards outside the Strikers box. Thomas lined up in the wall with Ben, Brad, Dean and Big Mac. They tensely waited for the kick. It was funny how the wall that looked so solid when you were facing it, felt slight and vulnerable when you were part of it.

Druitt took the kick diagonally across the wall trying to link up with Larson, but Mac broke from the end of the wall and harried the forward. Larson still got a foot to it and managed to flick it goalwards but Sean Pincher had it well covered. He picked up and hurled a long throw out to Cosimo Lagattello on the right. Cosimo took an age on the ball and Drew Stilton screamed at him to release it. Finally he was caught in possession and robbed. A first-time pass dropped to the feet of Carl Larson again who had darted in unmarked – Thomas was attending to Turveinen, out on the wing. Larson took the ball ten yards and suddenly saw his opportunity and shot hard and low. The ball swung viciously and Sean Pincher who was off his line was well beaten. The Mersey crowd was already going up for a goal when Dave Franchi, who had positioned himself on the far post, headed off the line. The ball looped out to where Thomas stood alongside the big Finn. They both went up for it together and this time Thomas felt the Finn's elbow in his face and pushed him hard. Over went the United wing back and Thomas cleared the ball up-field. Immediately the United supporters reacted.

> 'Headley
> Watch your head.
> When we get you
> You're dead!'

Thomas felt his temper rise. The United forwards had been kicking him up in the air all afternoon. But he resisted the temptation to react and ignored the jibes of the crowd. 'Be "Cool Tom",' Elaine was always saying to him. 'Whether they're loving you or hating you, don't let it get to you. Turn your anger into energy.' He knew she was right. But it was difficult. Sometimes he didn't feel like 'Cool Tom' at all.

Strikers were slowly taking control of the game now and the Demons settled back behind the ball to defend in numbers. Thomas took a much needed breather. He looked on as Turveinen was brought down by a fierce tackle by Big Mac and couldn't help feeling that it served him right as the whistle shrilled and Turveinen limped from the field after the collision. On came Arnold 'Iron' Brew, one of Mersey United's craggy midfield veterans with a reputation for uncompromising tackling.

Joss Morecombe matched that with his own substitution. He called in Cozzie Lagattello and gave young Paul Bosch a chance to show his skills. Thomas glanced up at the board. Twenty minutes to go – anything could still happen. He started to move into slightly more attacking positions – though never taking his eye off Larson and always looking for cover from Brad Trainor.

He nearly got caught on the break by a long ball from Brew and old Doolally again rushed up to the touchline to remonstrate with him. Another encounter with Larson and Druitt saw Thomas sandwiched and stamped on. This time he got the free kick, but as he got to his feet he reflected on the joys of being a defender; he had never been so battered and bruised in a game in all his life.

Finally the ref produced the first yellow card of the game for another dangerous challenge by Brew. He could have given four or five if he'd kept his eyes on things. It was still 0–0 and the match slipped into injury time. With the ref already glancing at his watch, Dave Franchi cleared the ball up-field to Big Mac. There seemed nothing on but somehow Mac got it through a packed Mersey defence to Paul Bosch who turned his marker and passed back into space for Mac to run on to it. Mac got to the ball ahead of two defenders. Just as it looked as if he was going to shoot he tapped a sideways pass into the path of Haile Reifer. The 6 ft 3 in Jamaican took a stride forward. Too complicated, thought Thomas. Shoot! The goalie made his move and just as it looked as if Haile had lost the chance he laid a delicate ball to the feet of Drew Stilton who had slid into position on his left. Drew slammed it into the top-left corner of an empty goal.

'STRIKER BABES TAME MERSEY HARD MEN' ran the back-page headline in the late edition of the *Evening Sentinel*. There was a picture of Thomas, taking the ball off Larson early on in the game, with the caption 'Headley shines in defence'. He wasn't sure if he was pleased about that or not. Elaine and Richie were delighted though, and Richie seized it for the scrapbook he was keeping on his big brother's football career.

After the Mersey United game, Sherwood were still tenth in the league. The Premiership looked like this:

	Played	Won	Drawn	Lost	For	Against	Points
St James	31	19	6	6	67	24	63
Highfield Rovers	30	16	8	6	60	32	56
Border Town	29	17	5	7	58	25	56
Mersey City	30	13	13	4	49	21	52
West Thames Wanderers	30	15	6	9	56	31	51
White Hart United	30	13	8	9	42	35	47
Danebridge Forest	29	12	9	8	39	37	45
Barbican	31	12	7	12	47	35	43
Wednesfield Royals	29	11	9	9	27	27	42
Sherwood Strikers	**31**	**11**	**7**	**13**	**41**	**41**	**40**

Mersey United	30	10	8	12	30	41	38
Southdown United	31	9	10	12	34	45	37
Kingstown Academy	30	8	11	11	31	42	35
Alexandra Park	29	9	7	13	26	40	34
Branston Town	29	8	9	12	34	41	33
Weirdale Harriers	30	8	8	14	33	46	32
West Vale	30	7	9	14	25	42	30
Burton Athletic	30	6	12	12	32	57	30
Fenland Rangers	29	6	9	14	29	55	27
Sultan Palace	31	4	12	15	24	60	24

Fame as a defender was okay, thought Thomas, but now he had his mind made up. He knew it was strikers, not defenders, who got all the glory. It stuck in his throat that Drew Stilton had been voted man of the match. I want to be a striker – or a creative midfield player, thought Thomas. And they're trying to turn me into a defender. I've got to do something about it.

Although he'd never been so tired in his life after a game, he went out that evening to Studs – the disco at the Palm Tree. Studs was the latest place for the football crowd, or at least for those who were allowed past the two big animals on the door and could afford the monster price of the Palm Tree's drinks. He was happy enough to sit and talk to Rory and Jason. They had both been playing in the reserves and had gone down 0–2 to Basingwood Town.

'I don't see what you've got to moan about,' said Jason to Thomas, who had been complaining about his new role as left back. 'You're in the first team, right? I wouldn't care what position I had if I could get a regular place.' Jason was making his way back from injury and it's always hard to re-establish yourself – particularly when other players are in form.

'And what about me?' said Rory. 'There's only one place for me in the side. In goal. And who's got that job? Only Sean Pincher, the best keeper in the country.'

'Can I join you?' said a new voice. It was Katie Moncrieff, the football reporter on the *Mirror*, a good friend of the young Strikers trio. Her cool head and quick thinking had rescued the club from what might have been a disastrous match-fixing scandal.

'Sure. Let me get you a chair,' said Rory who was always the polite one. The other two didn't move from their seats. Across the dimly lit room, Pete Frame, the Strikers press officer, glanced up. Unlike the players, he was on duty. Joss Morecombe made sure that someone from the club was always around when his young stars gathered in public. When Pete saw it was Katie they were with, he sat back. If someone like Barney Haggard, the sensation-seeking radio commentator, had tried to muscle in on the lads, he would have found it impossible to get rid of the smooth-talking Pete.

'I need to get some speed,' said Thomas. 'I'm getting fat and slow. Don't quote me,' he added, remembering Katie's job. Suddenly he recalled something she had once said to him. 'You're a runner, aren't you?' he asked her.

'Well, I was. I'm retired now,' she laughed.

'Seriously, I need to run faster. I've got to build up my speed,' said Thomas.

'Me too,' said Jason.

'Don't make me laugh,' said Rory. Jason had a bad reputation for skipping training.

'If you want speed,' said Katie, 'you need Doc Martin.'

'Shoes won't make any difference,' said Jason.

'Doc Martin not Doc Martens,' said Katie. 'When I came down here from Scotland, I was still thinking seriously about running, and I trained with him. He's fantastic. A bit of a nutter some would say. He lives on raisins and broccoli and things like that. He runs a gym out at Pyle's Castle. He specializes in sprinters. Have you heard of Shula Rowton?'

'Nope.'

'She's the European Under-18 100 metres champion. She trains with him.'

'I wanna meet him,' said Thomas.

'Maybe I should too,' said Jason.

'You're so dynamic, Jace,' said Rory with a laugh.

'I'll fix it,' said Katie. 'Leave it to me. And how do you like the idea of a new owner, by the way?'

'Eh?'

'Haven't you heard? Redman Forster is supposed to be trying to buy Sherwood Strikers.'

'Who's Redman Forster?' asked Thomas.

'Oh, just the owner of about half the TV stations in the world, not to mention three daily newspapers in the UK alone. Not mine, though.'

'I thought Monty Windsor owned Strikers,' said Thomas.

'Sort of. The Windsor family's controlled the club for years. But it's bigger than them now and the board wants more success – success in Europe – and that means a bigger squad. Even though Strikers is one of the richest teams in the Premiership, it needs to raise more cash and Monty hasn't got it. But Redman has. Redman could buy ten Sherwood Strikers without blinking.'

'Does it matter who owns the club?' said Jason with a yawn.

'We could do with a few new players. Especially defenders,' said Thomas.

'I think it matters a lot who owns the club,' said Katie seriously. 'Strikers is one of the top five, maybe top three, clubs in the country. I don't like to think of them becoming Redman Forster's property.'

'The top one,' said Rory stoutly, and she laughed.

'Let's talk about something else. After all, it's what happens on the field that matters,' said Thomas.

CHAPTER THREE

STEPPING UP THE PACE

'Bor-ing, bor-ing.'

The cry rolled around the terraces of Compton Fields. The Strikers fans were down in force to support the Reds in the fourth round of the League Cup semi-final. The chant was an old favourite and it hadn't taken long for Strikers fans to launch into the traditional taunt: 'Bor-ing Barbican'. Not that Barbican were so boring these days. For a start they had scored six more goals than Strikers this season in the Premiership and the Reds had a reputation for being an attacking side. Barbican had a new manager and he had brought together a midfield trio who could lay claim to being the best in the country. But old reputations die hard.

Only a few minutes into the game, the home-team sweeper kicked the ball back from the halfway line to his keeper and the Strikers fans groaned noisily. Thomas couldn't help grinning. But he knew Barbican were no pushover. Their manager, Albert LaBarbe, had made the side into a formidable unit with organization and cohesion and real pace up front. They did not, however, have the creative dash of St James or the attacking instincts of Strikers or Highfield Rovers. 'Slow and steady' could have been their motto. At the time that Strikers had bought Thomas, Barbican had also been interested. He was glad that Joss Morecombe had beaten LaBarbe to it. Joss believed that football should be exciting and passionate, and Thomas agreed. But playing for the Barbican set-up wouldn't have been a bad second choice.

The patient build-up favoured by Barbican was a tough challenge to any defence. It took concentration to counter it. On the back line with Thomas today were Dean Oldie, Dave Franchi and Brad Trainor, all of them with years of experience.

'Watch oot fir Deano, Tommeh,' the skipper had said. 'He kens how tae deal wi' the Archers. Gang whar he tells ye.'

Obediently, Thomas placed himself where Dean directed. Compared with the United game it seemed a very static affair as both sides waited for mistakes. But the orders were clear. Mark your man, cover for each other, be alert for the breakaway.

He watched intently as an attacking movement developed from the halfway line. Stacey, the Barbican captain, dodged a wild tackle by Drew Stilton and rolled the ball out to the left wing. The Barbican midfield then played a series of neat little triangular build-ups down the left –

switching the angles and seeking an opening. As if moved by strings, the Reds defence moved together to counter the developing attack. The Barbican midfield trio of Maschak, Clooney and Grandet passed the ball back and forth with deceptive ease, holding possession at all costs. But then suddenly the tempo changed. Maschak was the arrow head. He darted forward, Clooney passed to Grandet and the ball went out to the right where Thomas was marking the big number eleven. He moved to cover him, when to his surprise he was elbowed aside by another Barbican player surging forward. It was supposed to look accidental but Thomas knew it wasn't. He had been taken out deliberately. Fortunately for Strikers, Drew was, for once, pushing back and he put in a tackle which cut out the chance of a cross from a dangerous position.

'What are you doing – messing about on the floor?' shouted Drew to Thomas. 'Let me know when you're going to screw up again and I'll come and sort it out.'

Thomas turned away. He knew that if he looked at Drew's stupid face he'd want to rearrange it with his fist. It took him a few minutes to calm down.

The pattern of play continued with Barbican having much more of the possession but not creating too many chances. Twice Sean Pincher had to come out and intercept crosses and he made one brave save at the feet of their number nine, Marky Mullett.

From the keeper's throw Thomas took the ball into the Archers half, then glanced swiftly up to see who was ahead of him: Big Mac? Stilton? Bosch? Drew was clear, and well placed out on the left. Reluctantly, Thomas booted the ball to him, and Drew ran with it before getting in a low hard cross which was touched away for a corner. From Big Mac's place kick, Paul Bosch had a clear header on goal but he put it just over the bar.

'Bor-ing!' chanted the Strikers' fans as play again became a succession of clever passes strung across the pitch; the Archers were controlling possession but seemingly going nowhere. The shouts from the home fans rose in opposition and then they turned to whistles as Clooney was brought down by Dean Oldie but the ref waved play on.

'Stand up if you hate Psycho' they chanted. Deano threaded a fine, long ball through to a knot of Strikers players on the halfway line and instantly turned and grinned at his taunters. They loved him. Even the opposition supporters got a buzz out of Deano.

Drew Stilton surged forward with the ball, riding the tackles. Suddenly there was a cry from the crowd and the ref's whistle rose shrilly above it. Someone was down in the area. Thomas craned his neck to see. It was Cosimo Lagattello, writhing dramatically on the turf inside the box. Was it a penalty? The ref consulted the linesman and the boos of the Barbican fans told Thomas just what he wanted to hear. In spite of the Archers' protests, Jamie MacLachlan placed the ball on the spot. The skipper usually took the penalties when Ashleigh wasn't around. The keeper crouched warily in front of him. The stadium went quiet for a moment. Then MacLachlan ran in from left and blasted it cleanly into the top left-hand corner of the net, past the keeper's outstretched fingers. A roar of triumph went up from the Strikers' terraces followed by the away supporters chants of

'Volare oh oh
Volare oh Cosimo'

and

'Big Mac
What a smack'

Being one down did not change the Archers' approach. They held their shape and kept to the method of steady build-up and sudden attack. The Strikers' defence had a busy time of it. Thomas found himself enjoying the game the more he was able to read the intentions of players running off the ball. He was beginning to build up a good understanding with Deano. Tired as he was at the end of it, he was almost disappointed when the final whistle went. The MacLachlan penalty was the only goal. Strikers would take a 1–0 advantage back for the home leg next week.

Joss Morecombe was sparing with his praise afterwards. 'A good result,' he said. 'But we let them dictate too much of the game.'

'Too many long balls out of defence,' said Drew with a nasty look at Thomas in particular. 'We'd have had more scoring chances if they had moved the ball faster through the midfield.'

The manager gave him a cool glance. 'That's not how I read it,' he said. 'I give full marks to the defence. They did their job. What I wanted to see was a lot more fire in the forward line. Right, Len?'

The senior coach nodded. 'Right, Gaffer.'

'The return leg shouldn't be too difficult,' said Dean. 'We've got them on a plate with that away goal. Good dive, Cozzie, by the way.'

'I no dive,' said Cosimo. 'He kick me up in air.'

'And you put in a nice little performance when you landed,' said Deano with a grin. 'I heard you from the other end of the pitch. Pavarotti would be proud of you.'

'Don't get over-confident about that return leg,' said Joss. 'If we play the match the way Albert LaBarbe wants, we just make it more difficult for ourselves. Like I say, I want to see a bit more fire up front. We missed Ashleigh today.'

Drew slumped back with a scowl.

Put *me* in the forward line, thought Thomas. But he didn't say anything. Towards the end of the game he had felt his legs going. He was short on pace and short on stamina. And he knew it.

'Thomas, you're going to be a writer!' said Elaine, with a smile of satisfaction.

'What?'

'The *Post* is going to run a Thomas Headley column every week. And they've doubled the money they were offering.'

Thomas was more alarmed than excited. 'How can I do that? I've just fixed up all this extra training, and anyway, I don't want to sit down and write. I haven't written anything since my GCSEs. And I can't think of anything interesting to say.'

'Of course you can.'

'I haven't got time. What's the point of Joss Morecombe keeping the press away from me when you make more and more work for me?'

'Don't worry. The ghost will do it.'

'Ghost?'

'They'll put a ghost writer on to it – a professional journalist. He'll talk to you, get your feelings about things, then write it in the way you'd have done it yourself. It won't take much of your time. And we see everything before it gets printed.'

'Ummm,' said Thomas, who still wasn't sure. 'Does the boss know about this?'

A serious look came over Elaine's face. 'Yes. I wouldn't say he was overjoyed, but he went along with it. It's one of Redman Forster's papers. But he doesn't want to stand in your way. A career in football can be very short and you've got to take your chances when you can. But, of course, there must be no criticising the team. And no secrets given away.'

Thomas sighed. 'Okay,' he said.

'I'm only trying to do my best for you,' said Elaine. 'I know you feel all these things crowd you. But it's not just the money. It helps your career – makes you an even bigger name. You need the publicity in football these days.'

'Okay,' said Thomas, pulling on his training jacket. 'Look, I have to go. If anyone wants me they'll have to come to Pyle's Castle. My mobile's broken.'

In the taxi on the way to the city outskirts, Thomas sat thinking. One thing he decided – if he was going to do all this extra stuff for money he was definitely going to buy a car. Elaine had resisted so far but now he had his driving licence – he'd passed first time three weeks ago – he wanted some smart wheels. Something really sporty but not stupid and flash like Drew's gold Porsche. The cab turned in among the shiny new buildings of the Pyle's Castle complex, which was close to the airport. He hopped out, and ran through the red swing doors of the BodyWorks.

'Ah, the great football star!' A little round rubber ball of a man, with bright eyes behind his glasses and a fringe of gingery beard greeted Thomas as he walked in. He was wearing a luminous yellow tracksuit and clutching a clipboard with a pen dangling from it.

Doc Martin was an original all right and Thomas still wasn't quite sure that Katie had sent him to the right place. Jason had pulled out after their first session last week. 'I don't need this on top of training,' he'd said. 'I'll be too knackered to go out of a night.' And Thomas was beginning to wonder whether he'd made a mistake, too.

'Have you been following my diet sheet?' asked the Doc.

'Yes,' said Thomas hesitantly. 'Mostly. But I didn't fancy all those green broccoli heads and the beans. They make me . . .'

Doc Martin held up his hands. 'Less weight, more energy. Training is only part of the process. We're going to put the spring back into your legs.'

'Can I ask one thing, Doc? What do you eat?'

'The same,' said the Doc wistfully. 'So I'm an exception. It must be the chemistry but whatever I do I stay round.' He rubbed his stomach. 'Mind you, I can still run faster than most people my shape. And, when I was a wrestler, no one could catch me when I ran away.'

In his first session at Doc Martin's Thomas had been surprised to find that he was doing everything but running. The little man sent him climbing ropes, swinging from rings, stretching, doing yoga exercises and vaulting. Each session was a work-out with a weird mixture of exercises. Today was the same except there were a load of electronic tests during the session. By the end, Thomas was exhausted, and he limply accepted a tall glass of carrot-and-tomato juice from Doc Martin.

'Your muscular co-ordination is exceptional,' said the Doc. 'Only one problem, I can see. You aren't breathing.'

'Eh?' said Thomas.

'Has nobody taught you how to breathe?'

'But I thought you just . . .'

'Sort of nothing. You need oxygen all the way down to your toes. Let's go to the weights.'

Fifteen minutes later, Thomas Headley's arm and stomach muscles felt like stretched elastic.

'Your lungs are part of your equipment, just like your arms and legs,' said Doc Martin. 'You have to learn to use them.'

Use them? Thomas thought his lungs were probably worn out – along with the rest of his aching body.

On the way back from the Doc's torture chamber, Thomas dialled Katie Moncrieff on his mobile. It wasn't broken. He'd lied to Elaine, just to get a quiet life for a change. He was already feeling bad about it. Thomas didn't often tell lies – especially to his mother.

'Hi,' he said to Katie. 'It's Thomas. I just wanted to say thanks for introducing me to Doc Martin. He's weird and his methods are a bit strange. But I think . . .'

'That's okay.' Katie's voice sounded cool and offhand.

'I really owe you a favour. I won't forget. Why don't we meet up at Studs soon? Or somewhere else?'

'Perhaps.'

'Hey, what's the matter?'

'Oh, nothing, Thomas. Thanks for saying thanks. I hope it does your career some good. You didn't do much for mine by signing up with the *Post*.'

'But I never . . .'

'You didn't even tell me you were planning to do it. We might have offered you a better deal with the *Mirror*. I could have ghosted for you even.'

'Listen, I think we . . .'

'Don't worry, Thomas. Some people are loyal to their friends, some aren't. Life's like that. I have to go now. See you.'

The line clicked dead.

CHAPTER FOUR

RAISING THE STAKES

The *Post*'s ghost writer was called Jeff Dickson. He was old and overweight with grey hair and a grey suit, in fact everything was grey apart from a bright yellow and orange tie and a large red nose. Thomas thought there was something tired and desperate about him – and his breath smelled – but he was likeable enough.

They met first at the press club at Trent Park and after that they usually spoke on the phone.

Thomas's first 'article' appeared on the inside back page of the *Post* on Saturday morning. The headline read:

WHY STRIKERS WILL WIN THE TREBLE
Thomas Headley tips Sherwood Strikers in record bid for three Cup competitions.

Strikers were one match away from the finals of the League and FA Cup and also in the semi-finals of the UEFA Cup where they would face Lazio. In the article Thomas said he was sure they would

43

win all three. That wasn't quite what he'd said to Jeff – his view had been that they had a fair chance if they could avoid injuries and suspensions. But Jeff must have heard it differently. It was strange to see his own newspaper article appear, without him writing a single word. Jeff asked the questions and Thomas gave him the answers – and that was it.

The players thought Thomas's piece was hilarious. 'Got any tips for the Grand National, Thomas?' asked Dave Franchi on the coach to the away game at White Hart United.

'Three Cups in your first season at Sherwood, Tommy,' said Dean Oldie. 'Where you going to keep all the silverware?'

By now Thomas was getting used to the jokes and jibes from his team-mates and learning to give as good as he got. And after they'd hammered White Hart 2–4 that afternoon he began to think maybe the treble wasn't beyond them. Strikers seemed to have hit a vein of form and everyone was playing well, particularly the front men. A goal each from Drew, Big Mac, Haile Reifer and Ashleigh, who was at last back in the team after three weeks out with injury, didn't flatter their performance. The defence was knitting together well too. That partly pleased Thomas – but only partly.

Jeff Dickson rang as soon as he got home. 'Great game, Thomas,' he said. Then he outlined the piece he wanted to write for the following Saturday. He said he wanted something a bit more personal. Jeff never pushed for information about Strikers or his mates in the team. But as they talked Thomas found himself giving away quite a lot about what went on in the Strikers dressing room or on the team coach or the plane when they were travelling to matches. It didn't matter much because he and Elaine always had the last word on what appeared in the paper. They could always refuse permission for anything Jeff wrote.

The fax of the article from the *Post* would always arrive on Thursday morning and Elaine crossed out the things she didn't like before sending it back. Jeff was a professional. The stuff he wrote was good – it was well written and it made sense, unlike some of the sports writers. And Jeff treated Thomas with respect. He was a friendly type who knew everything about football and practically everyone in it. So it was no surprise to Thomas when Jeff asked him along to lunch on Monday to meet a friend of his. Thomas wasn't busy so he agreed.

'Thomas, this is Ed Cuthbert, a mate of mine.'

Ed Cuthbert looked a bit like Cosimo Lagattello, tall, dark, trace of a beard. His suit looked even more expensive than the hideous ones Cozzie bought and Thomas knew that they cost over £4,000 a time.

'Hi, Thomas,' he said. 'Good to meet you. I'm part of Redman Forster's personal office team – his British office, that is. I just want to say, we like your column a lot. It's cool. Just what we need to sell papers. The two of you are doing a fantastic job. The readers love it. And, let me tell you, Redman – Mr Forster – he loves it too. He'd like to meet you, Thomas. What do you say?'

Thomas hesitated. He didn't like this man and he was beginning to feel a bit annoyed with Jeff for bringing him here. Ed continued, 'Redman'll be in town tomorrow. He's got business interests all over the globe but he flies in tonight and he wants to catch a Strikers game. Hey, did I tell you, he's a big Strikers fan? So what do you say to a chance of meeting the great man? Tomorrow. Let's say 10 am?'

'I'll be training. What about the afternoon?' said Thomas.

'Impossible. If Redman says . . .' began Ed, then he grinned. 'You're not a kid player, you can take a bit of time out, can't you, Thomas? Most people would walk over hot cinders to get a private meeting with Redman Forster.'

In the end Thomas agreed – if only to stop Ed telling him again how wonderful Redman Forster was. He was doing plenty of training at Pyle's Castle these days – so he could afford to miss out on half a session.

The rest of the lunch was rather boring with Ed talking a lot – mainly about what a cool newspaper the *Post* was and how cool it must be to play for Sherwood Strikers. Jeff hardly spoke.

Finally, just as they were about to leave, Ed said 'Oh, one thing, Thomas. It would be cool if you didn't tell anyone where you're going tomorrow. I'm thinking of you in saying that. With this take-over business going on and you talking to Redman – well, some people might put two and two together and make six – if you see what I mean.' He laughed gently, got up, tapped Thomas and Jeff on the shoulder, and was gone. Jeff sighed and seemed to come back to life again.

'Okay, Thomas, let's get down to important things. I need to check a couple of things in your article for this week. I've written most of it already so you'll have plenty of time to check it out.' Thomas got the feeling that Jeff was no great fan of Ed Cuthbert, or Redman Forster for that matter. So why had he arranged the lunch? There was something about the whole set-up that Thomas Headley did not like.

Tuesday morning came around quicker than Thomas wanted. He phoned Len Dallal about being late for training and old Doolally swore and told him to wake his ideas up or he'd be out of the side. Then Thomas called a taxi to take him to the Hildebrand, the five-star hotel where Redman Forster was staying.

'You're Thomas Headley, aren't you?' said the driver. 'Recognize you from the papers. Off to the Hildebrand, are you? Hope you've brought your cheque book. It'd take me a week to save up for one of their cups of coffee.'

When he stepped into the the ten-storey, stain-less steel atrium of the Hildebrand, he immediately recognized Ed Cuthbert in another flash suit. 'Let's go,' said Ed with his just-too-broad smile, and led Thomas across to a lift marked 'Penthouse Only'.

'Redman Forster doesn't live here, does he?' asked Thomas.

Ed smiled. 'No, this is just our base camp for the Strikers operation. Redman has homes in London, Los Angeles, Mexico and Melbourne. But mostly he lives on his plane.'

The lift opened onto the roof of the building. It was amazing. Something between a garden, a nightclub and a museum. Greek statues stood among the shrubs. The two biggest statues faced each other on either side of a large double door. Ed Cuthbert opened the door and beckoned to Thomas who followed him into a room with huge glass-panel windows on three sides. The view over Sherwood was spectacular – so spectacular that it was a few moments before Thomas noticed, across the room, the back of a huge man who seemed to be looking out over the town in the direction of the Trent Park ground.

Ed Cuthbert coughed, politely. The big man swung round, with a black-eyebrowed scowl.

'Aha!' His expression changed to a smile of welcome. 'So this is our man, er, Joseph?'

'Thomas,' murmured Ed.

'Yes – Thomas Headley!' He was the biggest, fattest man Thomas had ever seen. He reached out and Thomas felt his hand vanish into an enormous paw.

'Redman Forster. Sit down, sit down, Thomas.' He led Thomas to a leather couch. 'Breakfast?'

'No thanks, Mr Forster, I've already had mine.'

'Call me Redman. Have another. I always have a second one around now.'

As he spoke, a maid appeared with a tray containing a huge plate of bacon, eggs, kidneys, mushrooms and beans. She set it down in front of the giant. 'Another one for Thomas,' he ordered, tucking a napkin into his shirt collar and beginning to shovel the food into his mouth without stopping to draw breath.

'I like your column, Thomas. Glad you're doing it. You did the right thing, coming on board with us. Have you done television? Of course you have. Like it? Of course you do. Get as much practice as you can. When your playing days are over, I can put your face, your voice, into every home in the world, Thomas. Remember that.' He began spreading butter thickly on the toast. A second tray was placed in front of Thomas.

'Eat up,' said Redman Forster, inserting half a round of buttered toast into his mouth and reaching for a kingsize coffee cup.

'I'm sorry, I've had breakfast thanks,' said Thomas. His mind went back to his 'Doc Martin' breakfast of oatmeal, raisins, dried apricots and carrot juice.

'I said eat,' grunted Redman Forster. Thomas found himself lifting a forkful of beans to his mouth. 'You know I'm going to buy the Strikers?' said Redman Forster.

'Yes. I've heard,' mumbled Thomas through his mouthful.

'I'm a visionary, Thomas. An idealist. I look at things and say, how can I make them better? That's how I look at Strikers. It's a fine club, a fine side. But why is it not at the top of the Premier League? Because it's nowhere near reaching its true potential. I'm going to turn it into a world-class team. Football's getting bigger and bigger, Thomas. I don't have to tell you that. The little men, Windsor, Morecombe, don't see it, though. They see the Premiership, maybe Europe. I see beyond that. Global football – Korea, China, Japan, the States, Australia, Africa – they all want to be part of the action. It's got to be a world game; a world television game with everyone paying for the big fixtures. I want to rescue Strikers from the little men.'

He turned his head and looked into Thomas's eyes. His great bear-like arm fell across Thomas's shoulder.

'What do you say, Thomas? Do you like my vision?'

'Urm, yes. Yes, I do.'

'I knew you would. And you can help, Thomas. I want the players, your team-mates, to know that the big time – the real big time – is ahead of them. Redman Forster will make Sherwood Strikers the world's top soccer side. They'll share in the glory of that. And the money. When there's a World Super League, Strikers will be there. You'll be part of it – the key man in my side. I know the other guys respect you. Though you're young they'll listen to what you have to say. Tell them it the way you see it – the future is with the Forster Corporation. Are you with me?'

'Urm, yeah.'

'That's my boy.'

Redman Forster stood up. The mountain of food had somehow vanished while he was talking. He reached down, picked up a mushroom from Thomas's almost untouched plate, and popped it into his mouth. Thomas stood up too, and Ed Cuthbert reappeared from nowhere. The interview was at an end.

'Goodbye, Thomas. Glad we have you on board. Keep up the good work.'

As his cab drove out to the practice ground, Thomas was deep in thought. Redman Forster was impressive all right. Thomas couldn't help comparing him to Monty Windsor, the club chairman. Redman was big and fat, and Monty small and fat. But apart from that Redman Forster was aggressive, powerful, while Monty cracked feeble jokes and talked about getting his knighthood. Redman had all the money in the world, and Monty was said to be in financial trouble. Maybe Strikers did need a vision. And maybe Redman was just the man to provide it.

CHAPTER FIVE

SPEED TRIAL

'Look at that! It's a monster!' Young Richie Headley was bursting with excitement as his big brother steered the shining red Saab Convertible up the driveway. Elaine looked less pleased.

'It's a bit flash, isn't it?' she said.

'Strikers red,' said Thomas proudly.

'Can I sit behind the wheel?' said Richie excitedly, sliding into the low-slung front seat as Thomas was getting out.

'It looks fast – and dangerous,' said Elaine. 'Couldn't you have got something a bit more sensible for your first car?'

'We've already got a sensible car,' said Thomas. 'Anyway, this is only for the weekend – to try out.'

'It's okay,' said Richie, swinging his legs out of the Saab. 'But why didn't you get a Ferrari Maranello? That's the tops.'

'The tops is right. Do you know how much they cost?' said Thomas.

'But you're a millionaire,' said Richie.

'Not quite,' said Thomas. 'I don't earn *that* much.

And I've got you lot to look after and the house – not to mention all your Highfield Rovers kits.'

Richie laughed. As far as he was concerned he had a rich and famous big brother and he wanted to be just like him – except he wanted to play for Highfield Rovers and England, not Sherwood Strikers. Perhaps, if Thomas wasn't too old by then, they'd play in the same England side like the Charltons and the Neville brothers.

'Rovers are second in the Premiership,' he reminded Thomas. 'And they have a game in hand on St James. We're going to do the double this year, you'll see.' Like Sherwood, Highfield Rovers had reached the semi-finals of the FA Cup.

'Second,' sneered Thomas. 'Rovers always come second. And that's as high as you'll ever get. Runners-up in the league and runners-up in the Cup – if you're lucky. Haven't you noticed, the Reds are on a winning streak? Eight wins in eight games.'

'Well you've got no chance in your semi-final,' said Richie. 'St James will stuff you. And we're bound to thrash Fenland Rangers. We beat them 4–0 in the league.'

'Maybe,' said Thomas, patting his little brother on the head. 'Does that mean you don't want to be seen going out for a drive with a Sherwood Strikers player?'

'What!' said Richie his eyes gleaming with anticipation. 'All right, if you insist.'

Sherwood Strikers were still tenth in the

Premiership. Although they had no chance of winning the league the prospects of a place in Europe again next season were looking reasonably good if their run of form continued.

	Played	Won	Drawn	Lost	For	Against	Points
St James	33	19	7	7	67	25	64
Highfield Rovers	32	18	8	6	64	33	62
Border Town	30	18	5	7	60	25	59
Mersey City	32	13	14	5	50	26	53
West Thames Wanderers	32	15	7	10	56	36	52
White Hart United	33	14	8	11	46	41	50
Danebridge Forest	31	13	10	8	43	39	49
Wednesfield Royals	31	13	9	9	33	27	48
Barbican	33	12	8	13	48	40	44
Sherwood Strikers	**32**	**12**	**7**	**13**	**45**	**43**	**43**
Mersey United	33	11	10	12	33	43	43
Southdown United	33	10	10	13	37	48	40
Branston Town	32	10	9	13	39	44	39
Kingstown Academy	32	9	11	12	34	42	38
Alexandra Park	32	9	9	14	28	43	36
Weirdale Harriers	32	8	10	14	35	48	34
West Vale	32	7	9	16	27	50	30
Fenland Rangers	31	7	10	14	33	56	31
Burton Athletic	32	6	13	13	32	59	31
Sultan Palace	34	4	14	16	25	66	26

Thomas Headley had never felt more confident about his football. Strikers were on a roll; he was playing well – though still out of position in the back four – and he felt a whole lot fitter than he had just a few short weeks ago. That was mainly thanks to Doc Martin and his strange diet and training programme. The Doc's latest thing was almost-raw purple sea kale – which was a bit like spinach only crunchier. Thomas had eaten tons of it and he didn't mind it really. The same couldn't be said for Jason who had started coming along to the Doc's sessions again with Rory. Thomas was convinced that his friend's lack of fitness was keeping him out of the first team.

'I'm shattered,' said Jason after a particularly gruelling work out with the Doc. 'I can't live on this disgusting grub.'

'You're knackered because you've been out on the town every night this week,' said Rory.

'I wasn't late last night,' said Jason indignantly. 'I was home by two-thirty. It's just I had to get up again at six for this madness. It's not good for me.'

'I don't get it, Jace,' said Rory. 'You're busting to get back as a first-team regular and yet you won't do the work.'

'Listen, I don't need to work out twenty-four hours a day. And don't tell me you don't go down the club.'

'A night a week. Maybe two. But not every night like you,' said Rory.

'He's right,' said Thomas to his friend. 'You're a bit short on stamina these days.'

'And, once Len and Joss mark you down as an idler,' said Rory, 'you'll be on the transfer list and sliding down to the lower divisions before you can say purple sea kale. Is that what you want?'

'Don't you worry,' snapped Jason. 'I'll be back in the first-team squad really soon. You'll see. That's more than anyone can say for you.' And he stormed out.

'He's right,' said Rory disconsolately after Jason had left. 'Sometimes I think it's me that should be on the transfer list. As long as old Sean stays in this form I'm on the touchline. The trouble is, keepers go on for ever. Pinchy still has years left in him. I'd hate to leave Strikers and I know I've learned a lot from Sean – but I want a place in the US team in the World Cup and I won't get one if I stay on the reserves' bench here.'

'Maybe the World Cup's not the most important thing in the world.'

'Who said that?' Rory looked round in mock surprise. 'I don't believe what I'm hearing.'

'What I mean is . . . we've both, with luck, got ten years in football, maybe fifteen. There'll be plenty more World Cups.'

'For you, perhaps. But who knows if the US will qualify again?'

'Well, I've had two offers and I think I'm going to turn them both down.'

'What?'

'Yeah. Scotland and Jamaica have asked me to join their squads. But I want to play for England.'

'How come you can play for Scotland and Jamaica?'

'Because Elaine's Jamaican and my dad is Scottish. But, you see, if I play for either of them I've got no chance with England – I'll be out of the side for good. Right now I haven't got a prayer of getting in the England team as a defender – not with the players they've got to pick from. Dave Franchi's got more of a chance than me – he's got three England caps already and even he's a marginal selection for the last twenty-two. So if I say no to Jamaica and Scotland, it's goodbye World Cup.'

'It would be fun to play for the Reggae Boyz – they've got a good team,' said Rory.

'That's what Elaine says. Mind you, she's biased.'

'So you're going to wait and take a chance with England?'

'I guess so. After all I was born here. England's my country and I want to play for it. More than anything I can think of.'

'Don't look so serious,' said Rory. 'Remember what the boss says.'

'What?'

'It's only a game.'

'Yeah. Only a game. And then he goes on . . . but your life won't be worth a used bus ticket if we lose.'

Rory smiled. 'The boss has got a way with words, all right.'

'So are you serious about leaving?'

'Maybe. My agent tells me the Blues are look-ing for a keeper. Ole Jorgenson is going back to Sweden.'

The Blues, West Thames Wanderers, were one of the strongest teams in the Premier League. But their chairman, 'Honest John' Trapnel, had an unpleasant reputation for the way he treated managers and players alike, and the West Thames crowd was definitely the wild bunch of the Premiership.

'You can't go there. I'd never be able to speak to you again,' said Thomas.

'That's tempting,' said Rory. 'But seriously, you've got to look ahead. Everything's going to change at Trent Park when Redman Forster gets his hands on it. How long d'you think Len and Joss will last? They don't matter to Forster even though they're the best duo around. To get his hands on the club he's been going around saying the management is rubbish. So, soon as he wins control of Sherwood, Joss and Len get the boot . . . and fast.'

'I hadn't seen it like that.' Thomas looked thoughtful. A Redman Forster take-over had started to look very attractive to him. But he certainly didn't want to lose Joss as manager. Joss had been his biggest supporter at Sherwood. And even though it rankled being in defence, he still rated the boss as the best in the country. Loyalty, loyalty . . . the word kept ticking in his brain. He wished things didn't have to be so complicated.

*

Thomas was very keen to show off his improved sprinting speed and stamina to Len Dallal at training. A word from Len might make Joss see sense about playing him at left back. But Doolally hadn't been at training for the past few days. Joss said he was away on a special scouting trip, which was unusual because Len hated travelling. Len's assistant coach, Warren Fitzroy, ran the practice sessions and Thomas didn't get a chance to show off his speed because Warren was massively into heading. Heading was his latest passion after seeing the big strikers of St James hand out a 5–0 thrashing to Mersey United; all the goals came from headers and Warren thought Strikers played the ball on the ground too much and didn't concentrate on crosses and heading enough. That suited Thomas. He was tall, taller than Ashleigh and Drew Stilton and he was good with his head. He took particular pleasure in rising above Drew, three times in a row, and placing the ball in the back of the net.

'Why don't you clear off and leave goalscoring to the stars,' said Drew. 'You know you won't get a chance in front of goal in a game.'

'Maybe you're wrong,' said Thomas calmly.

'Oh, the donkey full back wants to be a forward does he?'

'If I'm faster than you, maybe I should be playing in your place,' said Thomas.

'Dream on,' said Drew.

'Then what would you say if I beat you over a sprint? Say the width of the practice pitch?'

'I'd resign. Give up football. Shoot myself. Who are you kidding? You've got no chance, Headley.'

'I'm ready when you are.'

They lined up along the touchline and Drew got a flying start by shouting 'Go!' before Thomas was concentrating. Even so, by halfway Thomas had hauled him in. His new relaxed running style simply ate up the ground between them. Drew began to panic. His arms started going wild and he lost his rhythm. And suddenly Thomas was past him. He reached the opposite touchline a good metre ahead of Drew and had time to turn and grin at the red face which was getting redder with rage.

Thomas smiled quietly to himself but said nothing – because he knew that would irritate Drew all the more. Drew looked at him bitterly. He opened his mouth to speak but then he spat on the ground, turned and walked away. Thomas couldn't remember when he'd last enjoyed himself so much.

CHAPTER SIX

BARBICAN AGAIN

The turning point was the home leg of the League Cup tie against Barbican. Looking back on it later, Thomas thought how easy it would have been to have avoided it all. And how different things could have been.

The first half was fine. At the end of it they were one up – a superb solo effort in the nineteenth minute by Ashleigh Coltrane. He ran half the length of the field after picking up a through-ball from Haile Reifer. He rode two tackles and a desperate effort to grab his shirt, rounded the sweeper, cut inside and, with only the Archers keeper to beat, swerved again. Just as it seemed he was running out of space he suddenly clipped the ball at an acute angle to his left. Instantly he was hit hard by the Archers' number fourteen and they both clattered to the ground as the ball slid into the net.

2–0 down on aggregate, the Archers started the second half in grim mood. After ten minutes, Joss Morecombe called off Coltrane, who was limping after another uncompromising tackle and brought on Aaron Bjorn Rorschach for his first game since Christmas. Two minutes later disaster struck.

From a Barbican throw-in their wing back took the ball down the left side where Thomas was dropping back in defence. He read the danger signs early. Three Barbican players had moved swiftly through the centre and the man marking by Strikers back four – Dean Oldie, Dave Franchi, Ben El Harra and Thomas – had left them square and stretched across the field. The pace of the movement had them back-pedalling hard. After a quick one-two on the wing which took out Thomas, their number twelve put in a well-weighted high ball to the Barbican front player, Mullett. He rose to head it as Big Mac came in hard from the right. There was a clash of heads which Thomas heard way out on the left and Strikers' captain hit the ground. For a moment or two he didn't move but by the time Thomas got to him Big Mac had opened his eyes and was holding his head. There was a cut under his eye and he looked dazed and concussed. The trainer came on and then the stretcher was hurried out on to the field and the Reds had lost their captain as well as their top striker in the space of five minutes.

Jason Le Braz came on to replace Mac and the captain's armband went to Sean Pincher in goal.

With Drew Stilton and Bjorn Aaron Rorschach up front, playing together for the first time, and no skipper to command the midfield, Sherwood began to look a shadow of the side they'd been in the first half. The Archers saw their opportunity and they went for it with their army of travelling fans in full cry behind them.

'Hand ball!' Ben El Harra had touched the ball away from the advancing Mullett just outside the penalty area and dead centre of the goal. The ref spotted it and Ben got a yellow card – he was lucky to avoid a red one. The wall lined up and Mullett himself hit a perfect curling ball from the set-piece which Thomas watched fly over his head and curl into the left corner of the net.

The Archers scented the impossible – the chance of victory. Suddenly Strikers couldn't keep possession. Every time the ball was cleared up the field, the front men failed to hold on to it and back it came time and again. Thomas could see that Dean Oldie was getting more and more wound up. The full back was always on a short fuse and, with Sean Pincher shouting at him from behind and the comedy of errors from the forwards in front of him, he was getting really niggly.

Finally he cracked. Mullett went past him on the outside and had a straight run at goal when Deano put in a two-footed tackle from behind which brought him down just outside the area. With Mullett clear on goal the ref had no choice but to send Deano off and he swaggered away in the direction of the tunnel to the baying jeers of the Barbican supporters. Barbican made a mess of the set-piece but the pressure continued on the Sherwood goal.

Even with ten men Strikers had one last chance to sew up the tie. Drew beat the offside trap on the break and was clean through. The keeper came out to meet him and Drew looked up for support. There was none. The number twenty-three shirt of Aaron Bjorn Rorschach was way back and Cozzie Lagattello was yards off the pace, running down the middle. So Drew went on alone. He dummied right, left and then went right. The keeper read him and dived at his feet before he could get a shot in and the ball ran loose to the Archers sweeper who punted up-field. The ball broke kindly for Mullett who saw Sean Pincher off his line and tried a speculative punt from fully forty yards. He timed it perfectly, and as Sean ran back desperately flapping at the ball over his head, it looped under the cross bar. The Barbican fans went wild. 2–2 on aggregate – and ahead on the away goals count double rule.

Strikers' second-half game plan was in tatters. Now they were forced to attack with a makeshift forward line and ten men on the pitch. Joss substituted Cozzie Lagattello, who had had a brilliant first half but was now being run off the pitch and introduced Curtis Cropper into the attack. That left the midfield dangerously stretched.

Barbican's midfielders took control of the park and the thin red line of Dave Franchi, Ben El Harra and Thomas came under increasing pressure with wave after wave of Barbican attacks. Behind them Sean was losing his cool and screaming at everyone on the pitch. Finally Mullett ran at

Dave Franchi on the edge of the area. Dave put out a foot and then withdrew it but Mullett saw his chance to go for a spectacular dive. It worked. The ref blew and pointed to the spot. All the Strikers players rushed round him to protest. Sean Pincher was the loudest. 'He dived, ref! And he was outside the area.' It was unusual to see Sean so animated – he was usually the quietest of players. The ref ignored him and the other protesters and placed the ball on the penalty spot. As the noise died down Mullett sent Sean the wrong way and ran the length of the pitch to celebrate his hat trick in front of the delirious Barbican fans at the far end. The unbelievable had happened. Barbican had netted three and now Strikers needed two goals to force a result.

It was never going to happen. With the minutes ticking away, the Archers sat back and killed off the game. The Strikers fans began to drift away long before the final whistle. And when it came the players didn't linger on the field to watch Barbican's fans salute their team.

The atmosphere in the dressing room was stormy. Dean Oldie had already dressed and gone home. Mac wasn't there either. Across the room, Thomas heard Drew Stilton's raised voice. 'Let down by our crap defence again,' said Drew loudly. 'They sat back like a bunch of Teletubbies. Never got the ball out to us. Never gave us a platform.'

Thomas had had enough. All the frustration of the game suddenly boiled up in him. 'That's rubbish,' he shouted. 'Why can't you admit you just played like a fairy on a Christmas tree?'

'What do you know, stupid?' sneered Drew. 'Thick defender Headley who can trap a ball further than I can kick it.' A couple of players laughed. Egged on, Drew came across the room, dangling his sweaty shirt and flicked it at Thomas. 'If you were any slower on the ball, you'd go backwards, Headley.'

Thomas Headley forgot everything. The red of Drew's shirt flashed in front of his eyes and he swung a punch at his head. Drew jerked back, then flicked at Thomas again with the shirt as if he were a matador teasing a bull. 'Come on, then big slow boy,' he said. Thomas pushed him hard and drew back to aim another punch.

'Pack it in,' said Sean Pincher, wading in between them and pulling them apart. A sudden silence fell over the dressing room and everyone looked towards the door. There stood Joss Morecombe, staring at Thomas and Drew.

'I'll see you two first thing tomorrow morning,' he said grimly. 'The skipper's got a suspected eye socket fracture. Oldie is a cert for another suspension. We're out of the League Cup. The fans are playing merry hell outside. And two stupid little boys want to have a fist-fight. Is this a football team or a kindergarten?'

'You can't win 'em all,' said Jeff Dickson reassuringly when they next met. Thomas was still smarting from the disciplinary interview with

Joss earlier in the morning when he and Drew had both been fined two weeks' pay. The boss, at his most formidable, had really laid into Drew and Thomas and told them that, if it happened again, they were both out of the squad for the rest of the season.

Joss's biggest worry, though, was the skipper. If Mac had a broken cheekbone, he'd be recovering for a couple of months. And Joss was in no doubt about the importance of Big Mac to his team. If he was out it was a big blow indeed.

'Anyway, Thomas, I've drafted something for this week's column. Tell me what you think.' Jeff's voice brought him back to the present. Thomas looked at the sheet of paper that Jeff thrust at him and read it. When he had finished, he looked across at his ghost writer. 'I can't say this.'

'Why not?'

'Well, listen to this bit for instance: "The time is ripe for a new approach at Trent Park. There's nothing wrong with the players, but is the management really delivering? In their day they were the greatest, but Sherwood can't wait much longer for the old glory days to return. A change at the top is needed . . . NOW." A bit strong, isn't it?'

'Not if it's true. It's what you think, isn't it, Thomas?'

'Well, er . . .' Thomas's thoughts drifted back to the disciplinary session with Joss and to Redman Forster's talk of Strikers in a world league.

Somehow he didn't feel quite so loyal to the boss just at that moment.

'The point is, it's what the *Post* wants you to say. And sometimes, when you're getting paid a lot of money, you have to listen to our point of view. Don't forget, Redman Forster owns the *Post* and Redman Forster wants to buy Sherwood Strikers. For the club's own good, you understand.'

Thomas nodded, but he didn't really understand. He wanted to talk to Elaine about it but she wasn't too pleased with him at the moment because he'd decided to buy the Saab.

'It's big business this,' continued Jeff. 'I'm not saying I like it, but I've got my job to do. The takeover could happen any time now that Redman has made an offer for the club. He wants to put pressure on Monty Windsor to sell. And he wants this to appear in his paper – and you don't argue with Redman Forster.'

'Oh, okay, if you think it will help,' said Thomas, still far from convinced. After all, he thought, Redman Forster's money would be good for the club. And what had they got to lose? If he hadn't felt that he'd just been docked two weeks' pay unfairly by Joss Morecombe he might have acted differently.

CHAPTER SEVEN

TEST OF LOYALTY

Early on Saturday morning Thomas drove into the car park at Trent Park. He had plenty of time before the coach left for the league game – away to Sultan Palace – and he wanted to try and have a word with old Doolally about his speed training. As he was getting out of his new dream machine he looked around to see if anyone was admiring it and noticed Katie Moncrieff also getting out of a car which was parked nearby. It was a rather battered J reg Astra.

'Hi,' said Katie, without a smile.

'Hey, what happened to the Audi?' asked Thomas, trying to be friendly and remembering their last telephone conversation.

'I couldn't afford to run it,' said Katie.

'I thought you journalists were well paid.'

'Don't you believe it. And anyway I'm thinking of resigning.'

'Why?'

'Because the sports editor's on my back all the time. He says I'm missing all the scoops. He wants more gossip on the players, more scandal and tittle tattle. And I'm just not that sort of journalist. I just want to write about football.'

'I'm sorry,' said Thomas.

'Not to worry,' she said. 'I may go back to Scotland. There's a job going in the Rangers press office.'

'Oh,' said Thomas. 'Don't you like it here?'

'There have been better times. Listen, I've got an interview with Pete Frame on this takeover,' said Katie. 'Can we talk later? Say half an hour?'

'Fine.'

Thomas found Len Dallal sorting out the away strip for the afternoon's game. He always liked to do that himself although he had plenty of assistants. Len was a stickler for detail which meant that he didn't trust anyone else to get it right.

'What is it, laddie?' said Doolally without looking up.

'I wanted to talk about where I'm playing – about being in the back four.'

'That's nowt to do with me and you know it. Talk to the gaffer.'

'I will,' said Thomas. 'But you could talk to him too.'

'Maybe I have.'

Thomas knew well enough that Len and Joss would have talked about him. They worked together and they discussed everything about the team. 'So what did you say?' he asked.

'That you were coming on as a defender and one day you might make a decent wing back.'

'But I don't want that.' Thomas stopped and started again. 'I've been doing a bit of extra training to build up my speed.'

'Have you now?' Even by his standards Len was being pretty uncooperative today.

'I've been doing a programme with someone called Doc Martin.'

'That loony! I've know the Doc for years – since he was a pro wrestler. He was cracked then . . . and he's cracked now. Used to throw referees out of the ring. I'm not saying he doesn't know a thing or two. But why didn't you come to me if you wanted extra training?'

'I wanted to build up my speed.'

'And now you're going to tell me you're like greased lightning and you want to play centre forward.'

'Well, sort of.'

'Then don't waste your breath. You're down to play at the back. And at the back is where you'll be. Understood?'

'But . . .'

'Now don't waste my time, laddie. I'm busy. Clear off.'

As Thomas turned angrily to leave he noticed a newspaper lying on the table. It was the *Post* and it was open on the inside back page. 'THE TRUTH ABOUT STRIKERS AND ME' ran the headline. Len saw him looking at it. 'Aye,' he said, 'that's another thing you'll want to talk to Joss Morecombe about. He's a big man and he can take your snivelling insults. But I'd call you an ungrateful little beggar. And, if I had my way, I'd kick you out of the team altogether.'

Thomas immediately went to find a copy of the *Post* in the players' lounge. He had forgotten that his article was appearing today. For some reason Jeff hadn't sent him the usual fax to approve on Thursday either. It was worse than he remembered, and Jeff had added some extra things after he'd seen it – including a description of Len Dallal as 'a man using yesterday's methods to build the team of the future'. No wonder Doolally was furious with him. It was like being called a relic and a has-been.

When Thomas met Katie again, her manner was still chilly. 'What's happening with the takeover?' he asked her.

'You tell me,' said Katie. 'I didn't get anything out of Pete. I don't think he knows much. Why don't you ask your friend Redman Forster?'

'He's no friend of mine.'

'Oh sorry – I thought you were doing his dirty work for him.'

'What do you mean?'

'Oh, come on Thomas, you're not that dumb. Forster has been buying shares in Sherwood. All the shares he can get his hands on. But, to get control, he's got to persuade Monty Windsor to sell his stake. Monty won't do that and he's far and away the biggest shareholder. He practically owns the club. But the rest of the directors know that Monty – rich though he is – isn't rich enough to take Sherwood to the top. It's my guess that they'll push Monty to sell, and the more Forster can undermine the present management, the better. And that's where you come in.'

'But I didn't write any of this,' said Thomas, pointing to his copy of the *Post*.

'I believe you. But come on, this nasty little article has got your name on it. How could you let them do it, Thomas?'

'But I . . .'

'The point is, every single reader of the *Post* believes that you wrote it and that you're backing Redman Forster to the hilt.'

'So what's wrong with that,' began Thomas. Katie just stared at him and he ended up telling her everything. He described his meeting with Ed Cuthbert and the strange encounter with the big tycoon himself. Then he told her what Jeff Dickson had said earlier in the week when he'd showed him the article. Katie listened intently, not saying a word.

'I suppose that's when I realized,' said Thomas. 'They didn't want a Thomas Headley column because I'm special. They don't want my views. It's all just part of the plan to get their hands on the club.'

Katie nodded. 'I could have told you that at the start. But you probably wouldn't have listened. People like Redman Forster only want people around them who do what they're told. Yes-men like poor old Jeff. Are you like that, Thomas?'

Thomas looked away.

'Because if you're not there's only one thing to do,' continued Katie.

'What?'

'Get out. Put some space between you and the *Post* as fast as you can.'

Katie wouldn't say any more and Thomas knew her well enough not to waste his time asking further questions. Their frank talk seemed to have cheered her up, though. 'I hear you've had an offer to play for Scotland,' she said.

'Yeah, but I've decided to turn them down.'

'Thomas, you're sad. How can you pass up a chance to play for Scotland?' She laughed. 'It's what I always suspected. You're a treacherous Sassenach, aren't you?'

'A what?'

'You want to play for t'auld enemy. For England.'

'You bet.'

'Then good luck to you, Thomas. I hope they have the sense to pick you for the World Cup. I would.'

'As a defender?'

'No, as a wing half or playing off the front men. Doc tells me you're almost as quick as me these days. The England side could use more pace in the midfield.'

'But how will I ever be an England midfielder if Joss keeps sticking me at the back?'

'I can't solve all your problems for you, Thomas. Talk to him. That's if he'll see you after he's read this.'

*

That afternoon Strikers went down 1–0 to Sultan Palace, the bottom team in the Premiership. And the result could have been worse. The four-man back line of Franchi, El Harra, Delmonty and Headley fought a desperate rear-guard action with precious little support from Strikers' makeshift midfield. They ran themselves into the ground to keep out a rampant Palace side who were battling every inch of the way to avoid relegation. But Sherwood had no plan, no cohesion. A top team like St James would have probably put five or six past them. The solitary goal came in the second half. A half-clearance ran out to one of the Palace forwards and the shot went in off a deflection. When things aren't going right, luck deserts you.

CHAPTER EIGHT

UNDER THE HAMMER

'Cozzie's asked for a transfer.'

'What?'

'So the papers say. He says he's homesick and wants to go back to Italy.'

Thomas and Rory Betts were doing their morning run. Grey mist still lay across Pyle Park, and there was a chill in the air. Thomas thought about what Rory had just told him. They'd only just learned that Big Mac's injury wasn't as bad as it seemed and he would be back in the side in two or three weeks. That was the good news; but now, if Cosimo left, the midfield was in danger of melt-down.

'He told Joss he couldn't take the pressure any more. And he wants to play in Italy again.'

'What he means is that he doesn't like the training, the weather . . .'

'And he's missing his momma's pasta.'

'What about his contract?'

'Two years. But they can't force him to stay – it

would be pointless. And he hasn't been in the best of form. When did he last score a goal?'

'Still, I like Cozzie,' said Thomas. 'He's a bit of a show pony but he's got the gift. He's still an Italy player.'

'Yeah, he's good – when he bothers. He just left off trying when the young players came into the side.'

Later Thomas found that all the morning sport pages were full of the Cosimo story.

'ANOTHER BLOW TO AILING REDS' ran Katie's piece in the *Mirror*. One sentence she had written caught Thomas's eye. 'There is talent a-plenty at Strikers but the team does seem to be a touch short on loyalty.'

Loyalty, thought Thomas. Joss and Len and Big Mac probably all thought he was being disloyal. But was he? Where did his loyalty lie? To Joss Morecombe? To Redman Forster? To Thomas Headley? I am loyal to the club, he thought. But he knew that was dodging the issue. He was going to have to decide who he was supporting.

For some reason Joss hadn't said a word to him about the article. He'd been expecting another disciplinary meeting at the very least ever since Saturday, particularly after all the Sunday papers picked up on the story of his rift with Joss and the management at Strikers. The old rumours about his dissatisfaction with the club began to circulate again and Thomas remembered Joss's parting words to him when they had met only a few weeks earlier. 'You might say you owe something to the club,' he'd said. So what was Joss up to now? Why hadn't he spoken to him?

On the Wednesday after their humiliation by Sultan Palace, Strikers had a home game against Fenland Rangers. The Sherwood line-up looked more like the reserve side:

22
Rory Betts

| 14 | 3 | 19 | 7 |
| Tarquin Kelly | Ben El Harra | Ezal Delmonty | Thomas Headley |

| 17 | 4 | 21 | 20 |
| Paul Bosch | Brad Trainor | Jason Le Braz | Drew Stilton |

23
Aaron Bjorn Rorschach

9
Ashleigh Coltrane

In the programme Joss put a brave face on the changes that had been forced upon him. 'Our injuries and missing players give us a chance to experiment with a 4–4–1–1 system which we used successfully earlier in the season and to blood players with the talent of Rorschach and young Paul Bosch,' he said. What he didn't say was that half the team seemed to be playing out of position. That wasn't entirely Joss's fault. Further injuries to Sean Pincher, who had sprained a thumb in the Palace game, Curtis Cropper and Dave Franchi, meant that Strikers now had seven first-team players on the injured or unavailable list. It surprised Thomas that, in the circumstances, Joss had not played Cosimo but he was probably trying to show the Italian that he wanted a team of committed players. The big problem was in midfield where, in the absence of Mac, Cozzie and Haile Reifer, everyone seemed to be in the wrong place and, to add to the boss's woes, Brad Trainor was nursing a suspect hamstring.

In Big Mac's, Dave Franchi's and Sean's absence Ashleigh Coltrane was the reluctant captain.

'I can't do it, boss,' he said to Joss Morecombe. 'I'm no captain.'

'Let me be the judge of that, Ashleigh,' said Joss.

'I can't do it like Jamie did it.'

'Do it your way then. The lads respect you. They'll listen.'

Ashleigh was the only choice. Joss had considered the idea of making Thomas captain or even young Rory. But Rory, sensible lad though he was, was not a permanent member of the team. And Thomas? Thomas was going through a bit of a crisis and it wouldn't be fair to give him the burden of captaincy at a time like this. One day he'd be captain but he still had a lot to learn – particularly about making a bloody fool of himself in the newspapers. After talking to Elaine about the article in the *Post* he'd decided to say nothing to Thomas and let him stew for a bit.

Elaine was in on the conspiracy. She knew her son – and she knew he'd work it out for himself in the end . . . given time.

So it had to be Ashleigh for captain – but in his heart Joss knew that Ashleigh, brilliantly impulsive player though he was, was not the man to weld the team together. All in all he went into the match against Fenland with a heavier heart than usual.

The game kicked off at 7 pm and it was screened live on Sky Sports. In a confused first half, neither side took control of the game. Coltrane and Rorschach were closely marked and couldn't link up with the midfield who played as if they'd never met before. The ragged play rarely resulted in a serious attack on goal at either end. Drew Stilton, in particular, was frustrated by Fenland's tight marking and physical play. He had three shots at goal, all from long range and not a single one was on target.

Ashleigh, normally so laid back and relaxed, became more and more tense under the strains of captaincy. He gave Paul Bosch a lot of stick for his erratic passing and moaned at Drew for his selfishness, which was fair enough, but not very productive because Drew hated being criticized.

The second half began much like the first. But then in the fiftieth minute Drew saw his number twenty being waved from the touchline by Len. He couldn't believe they were pulling him off! Boris Poniowski was limbering up on the line and as he came on Drew stormed off the field.

Sixteen minutes into the half, Brad Trainor sliced an attempt to clear from the dead-ball line and skewed the ball to the feet of a Fenland forward bearing down on the six-yard box. Rory didn't have a chance as he blasted home. Joss Morecombe put his head in his hands, then remembered that the TV cameras would be on him, and resumed his usual poker-faced expression. The shock of the gifted goal took the stuffing out of the Reds for a few minutes and they could have gone a further two goals down if Rory had not pulled off a couple of remarkable saves.

At the other end Ashleigh Coltrane and Paul Bosch both failed to get the ball on target when a couple of half-chances fell their way. After the second of these the Fenland keeper, Jarvic, hurled the ball out down the middle and Bazza Taylor, their sweeper, chested it down and passed it out to the left wing where their number six took off like a greyhound. Most of the attacks were now going down the left because Thomas had both the wide players on the right well beaten for pace. All the time Bazza Taylor was keeping up with the ball down the centre. Thomas spotted his run and darted in from the right to provide cover. The cross came over his head and found the number eight in acres of space with the whole defence wrong-footed. Thomas hesitated. The number eight swung the ball in behind him where Bazza Taylor met it with the perfect header – down and across Rory.

0–2 down at home and the Reds' fans were

streaming out of the gates with a full fifteen minutes to play. No one could argue with that – the last quarter of an hour was probably the worst Thomas had ever seen at Trent Park. Fenland, like true relegation strugglers, sat back on their two-goal lead. Even so, they very nearly let Strikers back into the game. Boris Poniowski missed a sitter from no more than ten yards and their goalie saved well at Ashleigh's feet – the only true moments of life from Strikers in the whole of the second half. Strikers had now lost to the bottom two clubs in the Premiership in the space of five days and their run of eight wins was well and truly forgotten.

After the game Thomas was relieved that he wasn't called on to do any interviews. That tricky task fell to Ashleigh and the manager who had to answer the questions of a smirking Sky Sport linkman whilst a faction of the crowd outside the press box bayed:

'Morecombe out – we want Redman Forster' and others chanted 'bye bye Morecombe'.

Thursday morning came around all too quickly for Thomas because he knew that another *Post* article from Jeff was due. And, sure enough, there it was waiting for him on the dining-room table when he came down for breakfast.

'At least there's nothing about Joss or Len or any of your team-mates this week,' said Elaine. She'd been furious with Thomas for passing last Saturday's article without showing it to her – but, like Joss, she was keeping her opinions largely to herself. 'It's mostly about your new training style but there's a bit here I'm not sure about.' She passed the fax to Thomas.

'The last couple of results against relegation candidates Palace and Fenland Rangers can't have encouraged potential buyers of the club. I know we've got a lot of injuries but even so, it's no secret that our squad needs the signing of two or three top players to give us strength in depth.'

'I'll ring up Jeff and tell him to take that bit out,' she said.

'Why? It doesn't seem too controversial,' said Thomas.

'Because, with rumours flying around about the take-over, the last thing you need is to be seen taking sides. People are saying that with Strikers' recent poor showings, Redman Forster has backed off. Well, I don't believe it. I think he's playing a crafty game and until there's some real news you stay out of it, my lad.'

'Okay,' said Thomas. 'Do what you like.' Now, someone he respected was telling him not to take sides! He'd had enough of take-overs and all the hassle around them. All he wanted was to play football. Even if it turned out that he was playing in the back four of a team of losers.

CHAPTER NINE

DERBY DAY

Meanwhile, the season went unstoppably on. Two Premiership defeats left Strikers wallowing in mid-table with little chance of qualifying for Europe next season unless they won one of the three Cup competitions. But their next Premier League game wasn't about points but pride. Playing Danebridge Forest wasn't a game of football; it was war. The Danes were the Reds' local rivals. Anyone who grew up in this part of the country was either a Forest or a Strikers fan and plenty of families were split down the middle. Derby games between the two teams were always occasions of high drama.

But Monday's away game against Danebridge Forest presented special problems for Joss Morecombe. First there was the FA Cup semi-final against St James to consider. That was next Saturday and Strikers already had a side depleted by injuries and suspensions. Any more injuries and St James could book their tickets for Wembley without worrying about turning up for the semi-final. But this was Danebridge Forest. Strikers couldn't lie down and submit to their oldest foe. They had to slug it out with them.

The take-over battle was still taking up a lot of Joss's time, too. Monty Windsor had refused to release his family's grip on the club and Redman Forster had increased his bid. The board was split. There was talk of walk-outs. The atmosphere of uncertainty was sapping morale. The players were unsure of their future and so were the management and staff – not least the boss himself. Thomas could sense their worries, but he no longer felt so sure about Redman Forster. Something the boss had said to him stuck in his mind: 'money alone doesn't make a successful football team'. Joss Morecombe lived for Strikers. For the fat tycoon, owning Strikers was just part of a plan to control world football.

It was drizzling as the Strikers' coach moved through dense traffic across the industrial land-scape that lay between Sherwood and Danebridge. And the sky was growing ever darker. The players were quiet and more tense than usual. Once again the match would be televised live and the eyes of the nation would be on them. The pride of Sherwood Strikers was at stake.

The game began under floodlights even though normally at this time of year they wouldn't have been needed. The drizzle had stopped, but the sky was still heavily overcast, and the surface of the pitch, though firm, was damp and greasy. As the teams took up their positions Thomas could see that Joss had opted for the hard men. This wasn't going to be a game for finesse. No hostages would be taken.

22

Rory Betts

14   16   7   19

Tarquin Kelly   Brian Robertson   Thomas Headley Ezal Delmonty

24   21   18   20

Lanny McEwan   Jason Le Braz   Curtis Cropper   Drew Stilton

23

Aaron Bjorn Rorschach

9

Ashleigh Coltrane

Ben El Harra, Brad Trainor and Paul Bosch were out for this game so in came Lanny McEwan, Brian Robertson and Curtis Cropper. The game started at a frantic pace but the action was mostly taking place just where Joss Morecombe had feared – deep inside his own team's half. The Danes hurled themselves at the Strikers goal with attack after surging attack but somehow the Reds pushed them back. Danebridge were clearly still smarting from their 3–0 defeat at Sherwood earlier in the season and time and again they peppered the Strikers area with high crosses for their big number nine, Jon Frohlich, to latch onto. Brian Robertson was no midget either. At 6 ft 3 in he could match Frohlich in the air and Thomas quickly realized that this was part of the boss's plan; that's why Thomas himself was playing in the middle of the defence too – to give them extra height at the back.

Rory was having one of his greatest games; he made two tremendous saves, one a low dive to the feet of one of the Danes' forwards that left him with a stamped-on hand and the other a masterfully judged punch off Frohlich's head when the big forward had for once got away from Brian Robertson and seemed to have the goal at his mercy.

Then, in the forty-second minute, another diagonal cross lobbed into the area. At first it looked innocuous as Rory came out to claim it – but Big Robbo hadn't spotted him and he went for the ball too. As they got in each other's way the ball ran free. Rory dived in an attempt to push it away from one of the advancing forwards but only managed to palm the ball into the path of Jon Frohlich. It bobbled a bit and he didn't hit it cleanly but he got enough on it to direct the ball over the goal line as Thomas tried to kick it away with a desperate slide. The referee pointed to the centre spot.

The rain started again but that didn't dampen the Danes supporters. They were roaring their team on and jeering at the banks of damp and bedraggled Strikers fans opposite.

'Frohlich-, Froh-lich
make it two
and make 'em sick.'

And he nearly did, just before the half time whistle. It took another brave dive from Rory to deny the big forward who had gone clear after beating the offside trap.

At half time, Strikers were not in good spirits. The players stood around moodily, eyeing one another but saying nothing. Defeat was hanging in the air once again. Joss Morecombe surveyed them silently for a moment. Then he dropped his bombshell.

'This is where the rot stops. One goal down means nothing. We're going to be different in the second half. We're going to hit them. I'm changing to a 4–3–3. We haven't played that formation for a long time – mainly because we haven't had the players. But maybe today's the day.'

There were murmurs of surprise. 'Aaron comes off,' he continued. 'Ben comes on at the back and Thomas moves into midfield. Let's see this famous speed of yours, Thomas. And Drew – if you don't wake your ideas up a bit, you're off too. I want some action this half from the forwards and, if that means going back and fetching the ball, then do it. Understood?' Drew looked away and Joss swiftly sketched out the new formation on the board in the corner of the changing room.

22
Rory Betts

14	16	19	3
Tarquin Kelly	Brian Robertson	Ezal Delmonty	Ben El Harra

21	18	7
Jason Le Braz	Curtis Cropper	Thomas Headley

20	9	24
Drew Stilton	Ashleigh Coltrane	Lanny McEwan

STRIKERS

Thomas Headley looked at it blankly. For a moment he could not believe what the boss had said. He didn't even notice the look of venom on the face of Drew Stilton.

A buzz ran round the ground as the more knowledgeable Strikers' fans immediately grasped what was happening. They saluted the new formation with enthusiasm and, for the first time, they began to give their team some vocal support.

'Headley, Headley
up front
he's deadly'

Thomas couldn't deny himself a little smile as he heard the new chant for the first time. Now it was up to him.

'We win 2–1'

The Strikers' fans drowned out the opposition for the first time with their optimistic prediction. Back on the bench, Joss Morecombe and Doolally exchanged glances.

'Well, this is it,' murmured Joss.

'With guns blazing, Gaffer,' said Len.

The rain was heavier now and the pitch was turning soft and muddy. But Thomas felt like he was walking on air. He had been thinking 100 per cent defence – now he had to switch his approach, change his game plan and concentrate like fury.

His first touch of the ball in the second half was marked by a thudding tackle from Frankie

Ramsay, the Danes' and England's centre back.
Welcome back to the front row, thought Thomas,
picking himself up. He tackled back, stole the ball
from Ramsay who was looking up to pass and
crossed it to 'Little Mac' McEwan out on the
touchline. Thomas held his line inside Little Mac
and kept moving forward. McEwan to Cropper.
Cropper to Headley. Back to McEwan again. Little
Mac side-stepped his marker and shot down the
left wing like a bullet. Ashleigh Coltrane was in
the middle. So was Thomas, trailing him by few
yards and Drew Stilton on the far side. Little
Mac's cross was probably aimed in front of
Ashleigh but he pulled it a bit. Ashleigh rose but
could only head the ball back. Thomas chested it
down and hit the ball before it touched the deck.
WHUMP. Everyone held their breath as the left-
footed volley rocketed into the roof of the net.

The roar of the fans rose to a tumult. Thomas
fell to his knees and in seconds five or six players
had landed on top of him. Five minutes into the
second half and he had made his point in the most
emphatic of ways.

> 'Headley, Headley
> told you
> he was deadly'

The Danes did not take the equalizer lightly.
The sudden change in the Reds' attitude brought
a swift response from their forwards. Rory Betts
kept Strikers in the game with another reaction
save, tipping over from a close-range Frohlich

header. In midfield the sides slogged it out – neither side giving an inch.

Thomas was enjoying himself thoroughly, in spite of the pouring rain. He was splattered with mud, soaked to the skin, but he'd never felt happier. Free to switch with Little Mac on the wing, to show his pace by taking on the Danes defenders, he had the crowd roaring on every move he made. Suddenly he was having a blinder – making charges off the ball, dribbling down the wing, passing to perfection, running into space and building up a real understanding with Little Mac and Ashleigh Coltrane ahead of him. All the dangerous Sherwood moves were now coming down the left.

The Danes worked hard at closing them down and in the mud bath of the penalty area it wasn't easy to take the ball past them. Strikers were running out of options. Thomas wasn't being man marked but two Danes defenders were switching the duty between him and Little Mac as they overlapped. That gave him an idea. As Lanny went down the wing again, Thomas held back, taking the defender with him. Then suddenly he took off, leaving his marker dead for pace and screaming at Lanny McEwan for the inside pass. Back came the ball and Lanny kept running. Lanny's defender turned to block Thomas who immediately sent Little Mac away again with an early pass to beat the offside trap. It worked. The winger got to the deadball line and crossed. 'Right, Ashleigh!' shouted Thomas. The big striker was in the air above the defence and he headed down viciously with full power. The keeper had no chance. 1–2. Sherwood had their noses ahead.

'slow Trane
slow Trane'

Ashleigh did his famous limbo shuffle by the corner flag to the delight of the fans. Then the exuberant Reds supporters' chants gave way to a chorus of:

'Head-ley Head-ley'

Thomas saw Drew Stilton far away on the right wing. He'd hardly touched the ball in the second half. He wondered if Joss would substitute him. But he didn't have long to think about Drew – immediately he was tackling back to help out the defence and bringing the ball away to the delight of the fans. When the final whistle went Thomas couldn't believe it. The half had flashed by. It had been the quickest forty-five minutes of his life.

'Thomas? Is this Thomas Headley?' The voice on the telephone was familiar, but Thomas couldn't quite place it. 'Thomas, it's Ed here. Ed Cuthbert. Can I talk with you?'

'When?'

'Now. I'm parked right outside your house.'

Thomas looked out of the window and saw a silver Merc in the street outside.

Reluctantly, Thomas agreed to see him. But he

insisted that Ed came into the house rather than meeting him in the car as the American wanted.

'Ed Cuthbert is on his way in,' he informed Elaine.

'Oh,' she said coolly. 'What does he want?'

Ed Cuthbert, as immaculately dressed as ever, greeted Thomas like a long-lost friend, and shook hands warmly with Elaine.

'You must be proud of your son, Mrs Headley,' he said in his smooth manner.

Elaine smiled but not a lot and she didn't say a word.

'Redman sends his congratulations,' said Ed to Thomas. 'He saw the game, you know.'

'He was at the ground?'

'No. On TV. Big screen.' Ed reached into a slim, shiny brown briefcase and drew out a folder. 'Now Redman's even keener to buy the outfit. He's promised to spend an extra £40 million on new players. £40 million! That's more than sixty million bucks. Think of the players that will buy. But we've got to keep up the pressure on Monty Windsor.' He drew out a sheet of paper from his briefcase and handed it to Thomas.

'How many of the players do you think would sign this?'

Elaine took the paper from Thomas and read aloud: 'We, the undersigned, players of Sherwood Strikers Football Club, believe the club needs the secure future offered by the Forster Corporation and we urge the board to accept the current offer on the table.'

'Redman wants the support of the team's key players, you see,' said Ed happily. 'We'd like to see MacLachlan, Pincher, Coltrane, Franchi and, of course, you, signing this. And as many of the others as you can get – although, of course, they won't all be around when the new management gets working. But you will, Thomas. Redman's got big plans for you. He sees you as a future captain.'

Thomas glanced briefly at Elaine. She said nothing.

'I'm not doing it,' he said calmly.

'Hey, Thomas. What are you saying?' Ed looked amazed. 'You're on the Redman Forster payroll. You're on our side.'

'I'd sooner see the club stay as it is,' said Thomas.

'What? Windsor, Morecombe, Dallal and all that old gang?'

'That's what I said.'

'Thomas, you're making a big mistake,' said Ed Cuthbert. 'Redman Forster isn't going to like this.'

Thomas shrugged. 'I've thought it over,' he said. 'I don't want to do the column any more either. It's not my column anyway, just another way of trying to push your take-over.'

'But you've got a contract with us. And Redman Forster doesn't like people who break contracts. Don't make an enemy of him, Thomas. He doesn't let people rat on him.'

'I think you heard what my son said,' said Elaine, calmly ushering Ed to the door. When he had gone she returned and hugged Thomas.

'I'm so proud of you,' she said. 'It was my fault, signing you up with the *Post*. That was the mistake. I should have known better.'

'Never mind,' said Thomas. 'It taught me something I needed to know. Something about loyalty.'

CHAPTER TEN

FRONT RUNNERS

TOP REDS COME OUT FOR WINDSOR, shouted the *Mirror*'s back-page headline. Thomas read it with enormous pleasure.

After their conversation with Ed Cuthbert, Elaine had rung Joss Morecombe. Within half an hour the big man was sitting in the same chair that Ed had occupied, listening to Elaine and Thomas's version of the whole story.

'I thought,' said Thomas, 'we could do a letter from the team, like he wanted, but sticking up for you.'

'Well,' said Joss. 'Maybe a players' petition isn't such a bad idea. As long as they support the right side. Redman Forster will break up the team. And it's a good team with a great future.

'I could talk to Katie Moncrieff at the *Mirror*,' said Thomas.

'Then why don't you? Talk to some of the lads as well and get them to have a word with her. Tell her what you all think about the take-over. I shouldn't take Cosimo or Drew Stilton with you but I think you'll find the skipper and most of team support us – even if old Monty's a bit of a relic. What they understand is that the board is on the ball and Monty doesn't have much of a say in things these days.'

And that was how it happened. Katie met Thomas, Big Mac, Little Mac, Sean, Dave, Jason and Rory in the press room at Trent Park. And the rest, as they say, is history.

Katie's exclusive story appeared on Saturday morning – and, that afternoon, the first FA Cup semi-final was to be played at the City Ground. The other tie – scheduled for Sunday – was between Highfield Rovers and Fenland Rangers. The 46,000 capacity City Ground was completely sold out – half to Strikers' fans and half to St James. With the support these two old clubs had, they could have filled the ground five times over.

The Strikers players stayed overnight at the five-star Links Pullman Hotel. After breakfast, where everyone was talking about the article in the *Mirror*, Joss called a team meeting in one of the hotel's many suites.

'Good morning, lads,' said the boss, his face giving nothing away. Next to him sat Monty Windsor. 'You all know Monty and he's going to say a few words,' continued Joss.

Oh, no, thought Thomas. He's sold.

'I've come straight from a meeting,' began

Monty Windsor. 'Well, not quite straight. I have had two hours sleep. First I want to thank you for this.' He waved a copy of the *Mirror*. 'I think it made the difference. And I'm delighted to tell you that Sherwood Strikers FC will remain free and independent of the Forster Corporation. And, on top of that, the board and I have arranged for a long-term loan of twenty million pounds with the help of our sponsors, Standard Western Bank. All of that money will be spent on increasing the playing staff to ensure that Sherwood Strikers plays a leading role in English and European football. My family shares will be put into a trust and the club will be introduced to the stock market within the next few months. Nothing else, is there, Joss?'

'Only that you're staying on as chairman and I'm still the manager,' said Joss with a smile.

'Yes, yes.' Monty wiped his brow and sat down to a brief silence broken by a huge cheer from the players.

'There was one thing Redman Forster didn't know when he tried to buy us,' said Joss. 'He said he would make Strikers a world-class side. But Strikers *is* a world-class side already. Now let's go and prove it against St James. I'd very much like to see the FA Cup on the mantelpiece again this year.'

The Strikers' line-up at City Ground that afternoon was:

22
Rory Betts

4	2	14	3
Brad Trainor	Dave Franchi	Tarquin Kelly	Ben El Harra

8	21	7
Cosimo Lagattello	Jason Le Braz	Thomas Headley

20	9	24
Drew Stilton	Ashleigh Coltrane	Lanny McEwan

Reserves: 1 Sean Pincher, 6 Jamie MacLachlan, 19 Ezal Delmonty, 18 Curtis Cropper, 17 Paul Bosch.

Sean and Big Mac had both passed fitness tests but were starting the game on the bench. Back came Dave Franchi, as skipper, and, the big surprise, Cozzie Lagattello. Cosimo had had a long talk with the boss about his future and convinced Joss that he really saw himself as a Sherwood player. Joss knew the Sicilian was difficult and temperamental but he yielded to the temptation of seeing how he would perform in the new line-up. To give it balance they needed more power down the right and Cozzie, at his best, was just the player to provide it. What's more, Joss didn't underestimate the unsettling effect that the take-over business had had on the players. Strangely, Cosimo seemed to have suffered from it more than most – perhaps because he didn't really understand what was going on.

In spite of their result on Monday night, Strikers went into the game as complete underdogs. St James had had a brilliant season; they were sitting on top of the league. They had narrowly missed the double last year and there was a lot of money on them doing it this season.

The sun shone brightly as the teams came running out of the tunnel to the sounds of a brass band which was marching off in the other direction. A great roar went up from both sets of fans.

'Monty Monty
give us the cup'

howled the Sherwood fans as Monty Windsor took his seat in the directors' box. News of the deal had already gone out on lunchtime television. Monty Windsor stood up and gave a theatrical bow.

The opening moves were cautious; each side trying to hold on to possession and get behind the ball. The danger man up front was St James's French international, Paul Claudel, who already had twenty-seven goals to his credit this season. Thomas was a big fan of the phlegmatic Claudel and spent hours watching him on video re-runs. He was brilliant, the fastest player he'd ever seen from a standing start and as strong as a tow truck. Dave Franchi had the unenviable task of marking him and, if Dave wasn't 100 per cent fit, Paul Claudel would make him pay for it.

It was Claudel who brought the game to life. Picking up on a loose pass by Drew Stilton ten yards inside the St James half, he took off down field, full of purpose and menace. He went round

Jason, turned beautifully between Ben El Harra and Dave Franchi – leapt over a despairing lunge by Brad Trainor and unleashed a twenty-yard shot on the Sherwood goal which thundered in off the crossbar. It was the best individual goal Thomas had seen all season and he wanted to stand and applaud. The tall Frenchman pulled his shirt over his head and ran to the corner where the United fans were chanting his name.

The battle continued with each team taking the attack to the other. The ball must have crossed the halfway line more than a hundred times in the first half with the struggle for superiority being fought out hard in midfield.

The ref, Harry 'Red' Cardigan, was well known as a disciplinarian, and he stamped down hard on the first signs of trouble between the two teams. Little Mac was up-ended going down the left touchline. St James's Argentinean right back didn't even attempt to play the ball – it was sheer intimidation – and the United player was the first to go into the book. He wasn't the last. After half an hour, Brad Trainor and Jason Le Braz as well as two more United players all had yellow cards – and none of them could really complain.

The Reds nearly drew level in the thirty-eighth minute, when McEwan headed the ball out to Ashleigh Coltrane, who headed on to Thomas. Thomas set off on a diagonal run across the area and then back-heeled a delicate ball to Ashleigh who had floated into space. He brought it under control and drove in a fierce shot which the keeper just managed to touch round the post.

At half time, Len Dallal, always alert, saw Thomas rubbing his leg.

'Are you all right, laddie?' he asked.

'Yeah. Just a touch of cramp.'

'Well, you're running like a stag today,' said the coach. 'I think you're faster than Claudel, and I used to think nobody was close to him. Great goal though.'

'The best.'

'Let's see you stick one in like it.'

Thomas didn't have cramp – it was his old hamstring injury playing up again. It had kept him out of the side for most of the early part of the season. But he didn't tell Doolally – he didn't want to give him an excuse to pull him off.

> 'Coltrane Coltrane
> give us a goal or two'

rang out the chant of the crowd at the beginning of the second session.

Within seconds Ashleigh had a chance to answer their prayers. He was put through by a lovely pass from Drew Stilton and should have scored, but to his disgust he shot just wide of the post.

From the goal kick St James threaded the ball downfield and eventually found Claudel in the centre. With incredible dexterity the Frenchman twisted one way, then the other to go round Dave Franchi and even as Ben El Harra was bearing down on him he swung a curling shot towards the top right-hand corner of the goal. Rory was left groping at thin air.

The big scoreboard made grim reading.

ST JAMES 2   SHERWOOD STRIKERS 0
Claudel 12, 48

The Strikers' fans had gone quiet. Twice – at the beginning of each half – the French international had spoilt their party. Now Strikers had a mountain to climb. No one had come back from two down against United all season. Jason lost the ball at the restart but won it back. He then found Cosimo outside him and he pushed it ahead to Lanny McEwan who had made a temporary switch over to the right. His marker had followed him and seeing Thomas in acres of space over on the other wing, Little Mac swung over the perfect pass across the entire width of the park. Thomas took it in his stride and went for the dead-ball line. He looked up. Ashleigh was there. Get some weight on the centre, he said to himself. The cross came over and all Ashleigh had to do was nod it into the net. In it went. GOAL!

The relief on the faces of the Strikers players was matched only by the fans who had found their voice again. The biggest roar of the day was followed by a rousing chorus of 'Conga Brava', the latest Strikers tune. It rang out from the terraces and suddenly there was a carnival atmosphere throughout the stadium.

With only one goal separating the teams, St James couldn't afford to sit back. They came at Strikers again and again. In a hugely exciting phase of play the Strikers players were battling for the equalizer and battling for survival at the same time. Once again the war was fought out in midfield, and Thomas was in the thick of it. He'd forgotten about his hamstring and was running everywhere – tackling, blocking, linking up with the front three and going on breakaway runs of his own. Then he took the ball from a throw-in and saw a gap opening down the wing. He heard a shout to his right and there was Claudel running in furiously to head him off. Thomas accelerated. Looking neither right nor left, he raced with the ball. The Frenchman's grunting breath was right behind, then it was gone. A blue and white shirt jumped out in front, but with a final stride, Thomas managed to flick the ball. Ashleigh Coltrane was there. He stopped, turned to his right and curled a pass across to Drew Stilton on the far post. Drew nodded it down to the feet of Jason Le Braz who was coming in like a rocket and Jason slammed the ball home without breaking his stride.

ST JAMES 2   SHERWOOD STRIKERS 2
Claudel 12, 48   Coltrane 64,
                    Le Braz 84

Thomas pulled up. As he watched Ashleigh and Little Mac jumping all over Jason, he felt a stab of pain. Should he go off to avoid tearing the muscle badly? Even Drew joined in the celebrations. No, thought Thomas, I'm seeing this one out. And he ran over to give Jason a congratulatory hug.

Now the pressure was on. Five minutes to go. None of the Strikers players wanted a replay. Their fixtures list was already congested enough as it was. Five minutes to get the victory. But once again, Claudel broke away from Dave Franchi who wasn't able to match the Frenchman for pace. With Dave stranded Thomas had to provide cover. Claudel stepped over a tackle by Tarquin Kelly and, with perfect balance, controlled the ball and bore down on goal again. Rory came out to narrow the angle but the money was on the Frenchman. Instead of shooting he chose to go round the keeper – dummying to left, right, left and then right again. The goal was at his mercy but as he lifted his right foot for the shot, Thomas timed the perfect slide tackle and pushed the ball away for a corner. The Frenchman turned briefly to Thomas. 'Where you come from?' he said in disbelief. No one else on the pitch could have caught him. Claudel knew that. And so now did Thomas. The slide hadn't done his hamstring any good but he could still run and he jogged out to the wing to cover the corner.

The game had just gone into extra time when Cosimo and Jason exchanged a one-two down the centre and then Drew found some space on the wing. He cut inside and passed to Thomas who beat the first tackle and had a view of the goal from about twenty-five yards. Should he hit it or pass? Drew had come in on his right; Ashleigh was screaming for it to the left. Thomas dummied a shot and immediately passed to Drew. It was the perfect ball. Drew ran on to it and struck, first time, with his right boot. The keeper couldn't have seen it as it flew hard and true into the roof of the net.

Thomas wasn't surprised to see Drew running away from him towards the touchline with arms outspread to greet the cheers of the crowd. Drew always loved an audience as long as it was Drew Stilton who was the centre of attention. But this time Thomas followed him. 'Great goal,' he said in Drew's ear as Ashleigh piled in from behind. 'Wasn't it?' said Drew. Typical, thought Thomas as he ran back with a faint smile – but the giant digital board said it all:

ST JAMES 2	SHERWOOD STRIKERS 3
Claudel 12, 48	Coltrane 64, Le Braz 84, Stilton 90

The final whistle went immediately after the restart. Sherwood Strikers were through to the final. With Claudel's number nine shirt over his shoulder, Thomas saluted the fans who had rooted so hard for him.

'Give him a kiss,' they bellowed cheerfully.

Not content with exchanging shirts, the

Frenchman smiled and planted a bristly kiss on each of Thomas Headley's cheeks. He was a true sportsman as well as a great player.

Joss came striding on to the pitch to congratulate his players. Thomas hadn't seen scenes of joy like this since his arrival at Sherwood, and he revelled in it. Yes, Strikers were the greatest. There was no other team to play for. Joss raised his arms to salute the crowd and then walked over to where Thomas and Paul Claudel were standing.

'Man of the match, Thomas,' he said. It was the first Thomas knew of it. The loudspeaker announcement had been drowned out by the roars of the crowd. 'And you deserve it.'

'Is true,' said the big Frenchman. 'He run like the wind in Marseille.'

'And you couldn't have picked a better time to turn it on either,' continued Joss.

Thomas looked puzzled.

'I've been sitting next to the chairman of the FA and Jacky Dooley, the England team manager. And I think it's fair to say that they were impressed. Very impressed,' continued Joss.

'What!'

'Yes – in fact, without raising your hopes too much – the coach's last words were: "We've got to find a place in midfield for a young talent like that." '

'Lucky I wasn't playing at the back, then,' said Thomas with a grin. He felt his hamstring. Funny, the pain had gone completely.

RESULTS
(Games before the start of the story)

Week 1 – Saturday
Sherwood Strikers 2   Kingstown Academy 0   Premiership

Week 2 – Sunday
West Thames
Wanderers 1   Sherwood Strikers 2   Premiership

Week 2 – Wednesday
Sherwood Strikers 2   St Etienne 1   UEFA Cup
second leg
(Strikers win
7–1 on agg.)

(The story begins here)
Week 3 – Saturday
Sherwood Strikers 1   Mersey United 0   Premiership

Week 3 – Wednesday
Barbican 0   Sherwood Strikers 1   League Cup
semi-final
first leg

Week 4 – Saturday
White Hart United 2 Sherwood Strikers 4   Premiership

Week 4 – Wednesday
Sherwood Strikers 1   Barbican 3   League Cup
semi-final
second leg
(Strikers lose 2–3 on agg.)

Week 5 – Saturday
Sultan Palace 1   Sherwood Strikers 0   Premiership

Week 5 – Wednesday
Sherwood Strikers 0   Fenland Rangers 2   Premiership

Week 6 – Monday
Danebridge Forest 1   Sherwood Strikers 2   Premiership

Week 7 – Saturday
Sherwood Strikers 3   St James 2   FA Cup
semi-final
(at City
Ground)